Aleena

by

Farida Kotochi Adam

Chapter 1

Who am I? Well, I know the basics. Algerian Muslim girl – nothing much exciting about me. My name is Aleena, Aleena Ayad. I wasn't like a person in any other household who lives in a house. I didn't live with a family. I lived – or in fact should I say I worked – in a workhouse, and, like many others, grown to believe that we were orphans.

I sometimes wondered how it would be like to live in a house, to have a bed, or to have parents or siblings. I was grateful for one thing though, or should I say, one person – Maddy. My best friend.

I was never told how my parents passed away, but Maddy was, and she thought it was all her fault. I dreaded it being on her conscience forever. She says she was young when it happened, and she was in the car. Her parents were driving and she was crying, which diverted their attention from the road, causing them to crash.

She was very lucky to survive, the matron used to say. But there was something I felt like Maddy was hiding from me. The day the matron said that, in these words: "You were very lucky to survive-you and..." then Maddy gave her a little shake of the head, and then she kept quiet. This was when we were nine-ish, I think. How I got to work in a workhouse, well, was something else.

When we were little, the young orphaned ones would be taken to an orphanage.

It was very nice there. There was this particular staff who was a Muslim who told me about my Muslim parents. But then one day she passed away. I cried for days. I didn't have anyone to rely on at all.

Anyways, when you became ten, you had to go work in the workhouse until you were sixteen, then they kicked you out. So, when I became ten, my friends and I had to go to the workhouse. I heard it was illegal – us working in the workhouse- that was the proper olden day things.

But Miss Moss – the scary one we all worked for – or in other words, head of the workhouse, managed to work it out with The Mayor so she could 'have kids living in a more civilised manner-without gadgets. Make ourselves useful'.

But even worse, every month, children went missing.

Chapter 2

"Wake up!" There are groans and yawns from everyone, slowly waking up. "Wake up before I get the cane!" Everyone scrambles, jumping up and grabbing their aprons and hats from the headboards of our beds.

We scrambled downstairs, hearing the boys screaming. I shook my head. They probably took their sweet time waking up. It's funny, you know. I love reading books about children in my position, working under cruelty and injustice, in factories. But there's something that is always (well most of the time) the same about all our lives- we all have porridge for breakfast!

Cold, lumpy, or not sweet porridge- every single day. I guess the cook often smiles in my favour and puts honey in my porridge. It's our little secret. If Miss moss finds out, I wouldn't be the slightest bit surprised if I and the cook ended up in the lumpy porridge.

We finished our food and ran for fourteen hours' worth of work. Miss Moss got on my very last nerves every single day. She was so pedantic. The tiniest trace of dust, she was already ready to cane me or give me a good telling off. She won't leave me alone. I can't say she was much good at keeping *her* stuff neat, so I didn't exactly see how she'd be in a fit state in exactly one month, which was to be the inspection with The Mayor.

He was to come to see how much we clean and scrub, stack and carry. We would have to work ten times harder. I couldn't wait for that!

"Are you excited for The Mayor to come?" said Maddy from behind me.

"No! Are you crazy! If my back won't break from all this work I'm doing it certainly will break when *he* comes!" I replied.

"Not *he*. *They*." Maddy pointed out.

"What do you mean *they*?" I asked.

"What I mean by *they*, are The Mayor and his son."

"How do you know?"

"I overheard Miss Moss when I was mopping outside the kitchen." She winked.

I heard a loud whoosh descending. I recognised that sound from many experiences before and grabbed Maddie's hand and skidded to the side.

The whooshing sound was miss Mosses cane.

"Who do you think you are, superman?" She shouted, and her cane came down hard on my cheek. I winced and gritted my teeth. Tears pricked the sides of my eyes, but I wasn't going to give in. That's the last thing I would do. Let miss moss jubilate on managing to make me cry.

"No miss, sorry miss."

"And you..."

She turned to Maddy, who was scrambling backwards. "Get back to work! Come to her one more time and you will get the punishment she got, tenfold."

Maddy scrambled to her feet and ran away. Then her deadly gaze was fixed back on me again. Scared, I turned around and carried on scrubbing the skirting boards, and she left with an almost triumphant "Humph!"

I collapsed onto the floor.

"Are you okay?"Maddy asked, standing over me.

"Yeah, I think." I replied, fingering the mark on my face from the cane.

"Poor you, imagine how great it would be to escape from here, away from *that* old hag."

I laughed. "Carry on dreaming." But then it actually gave me the idea, something that would change my life forever.

Chapter 3

"Hmmm!" I was sweeping up the rubbish and looked up to see none other than...The Mayor.
He was fancily dressed in a top hat, a very curly moustache, a black suit and polished shoes. I got up to say "good morning Sir!" when he pushed my shoulder down swiftly with his middle and index finger.
"Under *no circumstance* is a child aloud to stop their duties!"
He strode off."

Behind him was another man who looked just like him, without a top hat, and much younger. He gave me a kind and sympathetic look and then smiled at me. "Steve – but you're going to have to call me Mr Stevenson." He said and put out his hand. No one had ever done that to me, so I just stared at it, wondering what to do. Shake it maybe? Seeing that I wasn't going to react back, he quickly retracted his hand. From the corner of my eye, I could see Maddy stifling a laugh.

The Mayor called him. "Steve? Where are you? Come write this down!"

I quickly curtsied like we'd been taught. "Aleena. Nice to meet you." I quickly said. He smiled, nodded his head, and went off.

I felt really guilty.

Maddy came running up to me. "You idiot! You should've shaken his hand!"

"Well, it's not like I've ever shaken an important person's hand before." I retorted.

"Well, I didn't know you were coming today! You said tomorrow! I'm not even ready yet!"

Yep. That was Miss Moss.

"Looks like you didn't get my letter in time and anyways, a good head that's steady must always...?" that was The Mayor.

"Oh, stop saying that!" Shouted Miss Moss.

"A boss that's steady must always be ready! Come on, you told me that one when we first met."

"Lower your voice...!"

Me and Maddy started to laugh. Then something else came to my head.

"Maddy, I was thinking about what you said last time."

"What did I say last time?"

"Remember? About escaping."

"*That*. I was only joking."

"No, for real. Imagine if we did. We could figure out a plan or something and find..."

"You're so silly, Aleena. I wish I had your enthusiasm. But your idea is going to be ridiculous. How much do we even earn? It would take weeks!"

"When did you tell me about the "*ridiculous*" idea of escaping?"

"Like...a month ago, as I said, it's not happening."

"Well, that's how long I've been saving up my money."

"Good for you, but look at the bigger picture. Anyway, remember, I'm always telling you how my money is always getting stolen."

I didn't dare to look at her, for I knew who was stealing her money.

"Actually, it was me- but don't take it that way. I was saving it for you so that you wouldn't use it up. I'm sorry. I guess I shouldn't have done that, but...look at the bigger picture!"

She grinned, and her eyes started to light up. I heaved in a sigh of relief.

"Let's do it!" she said, her eyes dancing.

"So, she managed to convince you into escaping, *sister.*" We swivelled around to see little

Matilda, her dark green eyes piercing into Maddy's lighter green eyes.

"Oh boy," Maddy whispered, her head in her hands.

Chapter 4

"Please take me with you!" Matilda begged for the fiftieth time.

"We're not going anymore! And especially not with *you*." Maddy replied. We were strolling on the grounds on a Sunday afternoon.

The Mayor's son persuaded Miss Moss to let us have a day off. The weather was beautiful, but my mood was the complete opposite.

"Stop lying! I have your money-yes gasp as much as you want-I can always throw it in the gutter, maybe chuck it in the fire - no, I'll give it to Miss Moss. Then I'll get into her good books."

I was fuming. Just *who* did she think she was. Just the type of thing *she* would do. All she wanted was a reaction from me and Maddy. I wouldn't give her that!

I looked at Maddy in admiration, who was conquering her anger so well. Calmly, Maddy spoke.

"Ok, whatever…fine." Matilda tossed the bag of money at Maddy.

"Here. And keep your promise." Maddy gave me a look, almost to say sorry.

"What did Matilda Mean by *sister*, yesterday." I asked Maddy, but she quickly changed the subject, so I just decided to go along with it. But I was determined to find out.

She dropped to the floor and patted the ground next to her. I sat down accordingly.

"Well, you are the first one out of all of us lot who know. Please don't spread it.

"She was just that annoying, embarrassing, mean sister. Unfortunately, life works like that. I didn't think you would want to even get to know me. I was going to tell you one day, that Matilda was my sister, Aleena. I knew you wouldn't judge me just because I had a brat for a sister. I just..." she let out a long shuddering sigh.

I put my arm around her and whispered. "You're right. I wouldn't have judged you." I paused. That's why when we were in the orphan care home, and the matron said: "You were very lucky to survive-you and your..." She was referring to Matilda.

That's just one big secret. Did she have any more?

"I promise I don't have any more," She said as if reading my mind.

"And you are always going to be my best friend. Thank you for understanding." I smiled but didn't say anything. We stared out into the open. Some people walked around in groups, some persuading cook to give them second helpings for their picnics.

"So, what's the plan for our escape." She whispered.

It was our top secret. We were dead if anyone found out.

"We need to figure out a date we're going to escape."

"And what about Matilda?"

"She's going to have to come. We know what we're in for if we don't!" And our first step to our escape had begun.

Chapter 5

"We'll leave in five days," whispered Maddy. It was night and we were all in bed.

 "Okay...but the most important part, how do we get out of this place? The workhouse is always locked at night."

"Well, there's a tunnel that leads underground. After approximately 3 minutes, you reach the stairs. You go up it and there's a hatch. It's locked from the inside so you have to twist the little handle on the hatch until it becomes loose. When you push it up you'll be in an alleyway, where the goods from our warehouse are dispatched. So, we're going to have to be really careful. Ten minutes away from there is the train station. I can't wait."

Her eyes twinkled with excitement. I must say, it was smart of her.

"Where did you get all this information from?" I whispered.

Just then, Miss Moss slammed the door open, making us all jump.

"Goodnight girls." And she actually smiled. This was not Miss Moss. How could it be? A great rabble broke through as she left the room. Everyone was shocked.

"Miss Moss is in a good mood." Jenny whispered to me and Maddy. She was a timid, frail little girl. We nodded vigorously in agreement. The door slammed open once again.

"Silence! Even one cough and ALL of you will be getting *caned*!"

Well, that's miss moss for you.

One question kept on lingering in my mind. That was, where are we going to go after we've escaped.

We're not going to be travelling from train to train for the rest of our lives. I didn't point this out though because I didn't want to dampen Maddy and Matildas spirits. I turned off the bedside lamp. "Goodnight." I whispered to Maddy.

"Goodnight." she sleepily answered. Another thing came to mind. Matilda was up to something, and I could have sworn that I heard her telling our escaping plan to her friend, Binky.

We would have to wait and see. Being December, the coldest time of year, many people fell ill. It was the day before the ultimate escape, but Maddy was getting more and more ill by the day.

She had been in the 'sickroom' for the past three days. I was getting worried as we were planning to escape the following night. It would be our last and only hope. The next day would be the tunnel work. That's why we chose the day before. The tunnel that was closed would be open in preparation. I went to visit Maddy.

"Looks like we can't scrub anymore because you're ill," I said dolefully.

"You will scrub fifty times harder, young lady!" Miss Moss snapped.

"Sorry, Miss."

We decided that scrub would be our code word for "escape".

"No, you scrub without me." She whispered back. She was very ill.

"You're joking, aren't you? You don't mean it...do you?"

"Of course, I mean it. Why waste such an opportunity just because of me. I'm being serious now. Promise me you will go. You have to."

Why was she so keen?

"Tell me what you're gonna do if I go?"

"I've got my own plans."

"I'm not going. What's the point of going without you. It's supposed to be our adventure."

Maddy sighed. "Ok, I'll sneak out tonight, but you better be there. I was meant to surprise you, but, oh well. Go tell Matilda I'm not coming. It might put her off coming too. Also, as soon as it is light's out go straight out, or I might miss you. That won't be good. Now, do you promise to keep to the plan?"

"Do you?"

"Yeah."

"I promise."

"Great. I wonder what our adventure will have in store for us." Maddy said, full of excitement.

"Shh." I whispered, getting up. "Bye!"

I went to Matilda and told her the plan.

She couldn't keep still. "What kind of friend are you?" She screamed at me.

"A really bad one who wants to escape without her best friend. So... I guess you're not coming?"

"Oh yeah I am. Maddie's annoying anyways. It'll be *our* adventure."

What? She screamed at me a minute ago for not being a good friend. And the way she said '*our*' did not sound right at all. Shaking out of nervousness and excitement, she asked in a quiet voice.

"Can Binky come?" I must've looked quite the sight. I could feel the rage flaring up inside me and my face reddening in anger. I clenched my fist. I probably looked like I was about to strike, and Matilda quickly backed away. "I was joking! I was only messing with you!"

"You'd better be joking," I said and walked off. What an audacious little girl she was!

Chapter 6

At night, as planned, we crept out of our beds. Binkies bed was empty, but I didn't think much of it. She was always going to the bathroom or getting a glass of water. We ran to the door of the tunnel and tried the handle. Yes! It opened. I looked back at Matilda, who was smiling like crazy. I took a deep breath in and opened the door. It was dark.

The only light to guide our way was Matildas' candle. She stumbled suddenly.

"Careful!" I whispered. The rocky floor continued as we walked in stony silence. The rough walls were blossoming with moss and a type of sticky segment. Water droplets gradually made their way to the floor. It slowly increased until we got to a patch of probably once dry mud that turned sticky and muddy. Hastily, we made our way through the mess until we got to the stairs. I looked back at Matilda, her eyes cunning. "Let our adventures begin."

"Adventure." I corrected. She was planning something. Why else would she say adventure*s*? We climbed up the stairs and went up the hatch. The hatch wasn't locked. Hopefully, it meant that Maddy had come before us. Maddy was standing over the hatch and helped us out. "The hatch was unlocked when I arrived." Said Maddy, closing the hatch. I looked at Matilda, who averted her eyes, but not quick enough for me not to catch her.

"What's wrong with you Matilda?" I snapped.

"What?"

"you're so... sceptical."

"What do you mean?"

"You're up to no good. That's what I mean."

"OK fine then. I'm up to no good. What are you going to do about it?"

"Let's go, guys. It's no good arguing with each other. If anyone is after us, they're going to catch up soon." Cut in Maddy. I picked up the bag that contained our monies.

We started following the sign post that showed where the strain station was. It turned out that it was only about three-four minutes away from the alleyway. My fears of the dark were haunting me though I forced myself to swallow them down.

The cold was getting the better of me. Not even the sight of the snowflakes slowly falling to the ground which we hadn't seen in ages could take my mind off it.

"It's rather dark. I wouldn't be surprised if any of us were frightened." Matilda suddenly said.

From the light of the street lamps, I could see she was trying to put on a brave face, despite her voice being shaky. She was in the middle of Maddy and me, so Maddy and I squeezed her hands.

I forced myself to be a bit compassionate, seeing as we were alone in the world now.

"Things are all going to be fine," Maddy whispered to her.

"Look, it's here!" I looked around, gaping. Our jaws dropped.

So, *that's* what train stations looked. I was nervous because it was night time and the chances of people staring at us and suspecting us were high, because children, all by themselves in a train station, dressed in brown dresses and white aprons? But this station was buzzing with people.

The atmosphere smelt rotten. I felt like I would become deaf from the sounds of the whistles.

"This is crazy!" Maddy whispered.

"Wonderful." I whispered.

"Matilda!" I heard someone shout. But before I turned to look, she was already trying to distract me. "What is *that*?" Matilda said, pointing to a spot of vacuity and before hurriedly retracting her arm from our hands. She looked unsure.

Maddy and I swivelled around to see nothing apart from a patch of raised earth, with a few wires piercing through and a black carrier bag flying.

I looked at Maddy. She gave me a disconcerted look. We looked back to see Matilda running towards a train about to leave. And she had the bag with our money. I wasn't going to have it. I sprinted as fast as I could in and out of the crowds until I got to her. "What do you think you're doing?"

"I'm going onto the train with Binky. Well done for guessing I was not up to any good earlier on," she replied, a nasty grin on her face. I snatched mine and Maddie's money out of the bag she was holding and tossed hers into her hands.

"Take your share. I don't even know what to say to you right now. We're better off without you anyways!" I screamed in her face. She pushed me back hard with great force for a little girl and ran off. I bashed my head on the ground and lay there in utter horror.

Chapter 7

"Wake up. No, please! Try opening your eyes."
I could hear Maddy pleading desperately. I opened my eyes. Seeing black dots all around me, I began to feel hopeless. I was cold, tired, scared, and nervous. I slowly stood up, with Maddy holding me up.

"Well, that was kind of dramatic. How did they not see her get onto the train? I'm sure she needed to pay for a ticket." I murmured.

We began walking out of the station, overthrown. My eyes rolled back into my head and my legs buckled underneath me. I fell forwards, but Maddy caught me, and we rested against a wall.

Wondrously, I regained full strength pretty fast, though I needed water. That's when I saw Maddie's face.

"Are you ok? You've gone green." I asked.

She gave a tight smile. "I'm fine," she croaked. "I reckon I shouldn't have yelled that much in the train station. I feel all funny, and my throats killing me."

"It was dangerous of you to leave the sick room in your condition."

"Your right."

"Do you think there was any point in escaping from the warehouse?"

"Yes. No. I don't know. Maybe."

"I know that I'll probably hate myself for admitting this ...I'm scared."

"You, scared?" she scoffed "What makes you say that?"

"Well, we've escaped from a warehouse. They are bound to be searching for us in the morning. Where do we go now? If we return, that would probably be the last time we see broad daylight again."

"Let's find somewhere safe where none can find us, and we'll sleep there. We're going to have to be sensible and not panic and reassure each other. That way me and you won't feel scared. At the break of dawn, we'll think of something."

So, we wondered about it, keeping to the shadows until we came across another alleyway. It was empty and dark, but there were no houses and a street lamp stood on a corner, hanging over a red phone box. We sat close to the phone box, trying to stay close to keep warm.

I woke up. It was just after dawn- it looked like six or seven o'clock to my untrained eye. I patted Maddy, but she didn't wake up. I lightly shook her. No response.

I was beginning to get worried because Maddy was a very light Sleeper. *I'll call the ambulance*, I thought. I stood up and looked into the phone box. That's when I realised I didn't even know the number for the ambulance. That's when I detected the piece of paper next to the phone. Was it somebodies?

Was I allowed to look at it? Although the location seemed deserted, I glimpsed behind me before picking up the paper. *If it's addressing anyone, I'll put it back.* Perhaps, just possibly, it might have what I wanted. I picked up the paper that seemed to be blank. I flipped it over.

This paper was a miracle. It had just what I required. It stated:

Police: two, two, four

Ambulance: six, six, six

Fire brigade: one, eight, three

I dialled the number for the ambulance. Immediately a woman picked up. I had to stay calm and not accidently spill out anything unnecessary. Should I say Maddy's my sister?

No, we didn't look anything Alike. I'll go with the truth. Some of it.

"Hello?" I said, my voice shaky.

"Hello. How can I help?"

"It's my...friend. She's ... I don't know what's wrong with her. She...we... I was walking outside with her then all of a sudden, she fell. I shook her and tapped her but she's not waking up."

"Ok, I'm just going to ask you a few questions." A few questions? My friend could be dying for all she knew.

"Ok."

"Can you tell me your friends name?"

"Maddy. Maddy Holsworth."

"Is she breathing?"

"Umm..."

"Can you see any movements in her?"

"Err..."

"Do you think she's fainted. Or maybe she..."

"No, no, no," I said, horrified. The lady on the phone gave a long sigh.

"Okay. We'll send somebody to you. Give me with the name of the street you are on." I glanced around hopelessly.

"Oh, summer trend Avenue." I noticed the signpost on the wall opposite me. I hoped it was the correct one.

"There doesn't seem to be a summer trend Avenue-wait-are you in London?"

"Yes."

"Oh. That's quite far."

"How far?"

"Half an hour."

Oh boy.

"I can wait...I guess."

"Are you sure?"

"Yeah."

"We'll try to get to you as soon as possible."

"Ok... Bye." Nothing.

Oh well. It's fine-I'm just sitting down in boredom for half an hour. Just then, Maddy stirred. I jerked. She gradually got up. She gradually got up. "Oh my god!" I cried.

"What?" She grunted.

"You've gone really white and pale. I don't think you're alright."

"Don't lie," she said, her face turning deadly serious.

"I called the ambulance for you. They will be here soon."

"Why did you call..." her words were becoming more slurred. "We can't trust *anyone* at the moment."

"Don't say anymore. Sorry, I guess, for calling them, but the lady on the phone really did sound nice."

We sat in silence until the ambulance appeared. They came with a bag filled with pieces of equipment.

"What's this?" They looked at her like an angel from heaven. They were clearly expecting something else. What's their problem?

"She woke up." I hurriedly said.

"This wasn't some sort of prank, was it?"One of the ladies said, narrowing her eyes. said, narrowing her eyes.

"It was hoax call," Mumbled the other lady.

"What should we have expected? She couldn't even answer the questions."

"It's NOT a hoax call. Maddy *just* got up and has gone really pale. *See.*"

"Oh, well, I guess she *has* lost some colour in her cheeks."

Do something about it then! Don't just stand there! I thought. After what seemed like hours of discussion, they brought a piece of equipment which looked like a plastic gas mask.

"We're just bringing you an oxygen mask." Gas mask oxygen mask-same thing. They knelt beside Maddy.

"We want you to breathe into here, and then tell us how you feel." They saw her face.

"I mean a thumbs up, thumbs down or in the middle." Maddy started taking deep, long breaths, inhaling and exhaling, inhaling and exhaling now, dear, how do you feel." Thumbs down.

"This isn't good, is it?" Said one of the women. At this time, I could see the uniform of these two women. Both were wearing dark blue trousers with white blouses and a white cap around their heads. I prayed silently in my heart, hoping they wouldn't ask why we dressed in those clothes.

They were nice enough, I guess. I just wished we were treated as well as we had to treat our dresses. *No time to wish though,* I thought. Were never going back again! "We're going to take you to the clinic, love. "Said one of the ladies. I looked up at them expectantly.

"Oh, very well, you can come too, but where are your parents?"

"They're out...on holiday. "

"How irresponsible."

I gave a triumphant yes when they had their backs to me. They helped her into the van ambulance- whatever it was and then got in themselves.

One stayed at the back of the van with Maddy, who had subsequently fainted again. I had to sit in the passenger's seat at the front. She seemed really scary as I went to sit next to her. I was busy looking through the window,

"Put on your seatbelt!" She snapped.

I jumped, gave her a look, and then put it on. I tried to make a conversation with her, but she put her foolish nose in the air and looked down on me as if I was a bare ant. She put on silly airs and graces.

She irritated me so much. I turned my back onto her a bit and she gave a sniff and a long infuriating sigh. I could hear faint murmuring from the back where Maddy was. I took no notice. I should've, though, for it could have

prepared me for something that would happen very, very
soon.

Chapter 8

We arrived at the hospital. The lady at the desk kept me engaged in a conversation until I got called to the room Maddy was in. Room Thirteen- some would say it's bad luck. I opened the door slowly and cautiously stepped in. Smiling at the woman next to Maddy, I walked over to her bed.

She was snoring contentedly, so I sat at the end of the bed and waited.

"Aleena?" the lady whispered. Her face was very stern. "Yeah?" I mouthed. She pointed towards a door behind her. I followed behind her and entered the room behind the door.

"You escaped from a workhouse. A warehouse I am guessing. Though why anyone at your age should work there I do not know."

She got straight to the point. I had often read books about kids in the olden days escaping from factories and little children escaping from bad families after being evacuated in world war two. But it never ended like this.

That was not me right now. And I couldn't ask for help. No one would believe me if I told them that I word for a scary old lady who made us work from morning to night eating the same thing every day *and* she was in league with *The Mayor*.

They'd think I've gone crazy. I looked down, my cheeks burning, wondering what to say. She sighed, took out her phone from her pocket and dialled a few numbers.

"It would help if you opened up to me a bit more." She said She was calling someone. No. No. No. I had to do something now, or I was dead if I had to return. She started to talk to the person on the phone. A man. I *had* to say something.

"How did you find out?" I asked desperately.

She said bye to the man she was talking with and put her phone back in her pocket.

"In the ambulance, Maddy was talking in her sleep. That's how we found out." I gasped. I felt a sudden surge of anger towards Maddy. It wasn't her fault. I know it wasn't fair of me either to be mad at her...

"I'm calling a taxi- it'll be here shortly to drive you back."

"No! You can't do this to me! It's just not fair!"

I forgot who I was talking to. Anger, resentment and pity for myself took the better of me.

"What do you mean?" She said, narrowing her eyes.

"Please act sensibly and go accordingly to the plan. "What plan?" I yelled, "There's *is* no *plan* as you call it and I'm not entering *any* fools taxi!"

"You need to calm down, and get a grip!" She shrieked. I shrank back. She was no longer a nurse. She was the wicked witch of the west. Her face was dark red, her chest heaving her fists clenched at her sides, almost as if it was to stop herself from hitting me.

I slowly turned around, to make my way out of the room, when she stopped me. I turned my face around, resentment spreading through me. She was much more composed. Her chest no longer heaving, her face no longer red and her fists no longer clenched.

"What?"

"Sorry about that. I'll leave you with Maddy whilst I go wait for your taxi to arrive- and I do *not* want you touching anything. And Maddy *stays* in the room. You hear me."

"Yes," I said meekly -though I had no intention of leaving Maddy- as soon as she was awake. We would get out of here somehow. Well, it seemed a reasonable plan. So as the nurse made her way downstairs, I sat next to Maddy. I watched her, her chest heaving up and down. I realised. *She's conscious. She's asleep.* I was about to wake her up, but something about her pale face and unsmiling mouth stopped me. I sighed and started pacing up and down the room. I had to think.

"Aleena?"

No need to wake her now. She was awake.

"How do you feel? Are you feeling better? We have to go now! The Nurse booked a taxi to take me back to the workhouse."

"I feel fine now. I think we should get going now."

She said, sliding out of bed.

"Oh, for goodness sake -there's a camera! Why didn't I notice that before!"

"So, people like you don't do silly stuff like stealing sick patients!" I was dead meat. The nurse was right there, at the door. I let go of the door handle. "Look, I can explain. You see..."

"No explanations. Off! The taxi's waiting for you downstairs."

"But Maddy! She's my friend..."

"Enough with your nonsense -or we'll have to take you by force!"

"Ok fine. I'll go." I said, glowering.

"Can I have a quick word with Aleena before she goes then?" Maddy asked.

"Go on."

"We'll see each other again eventually, I hope," she whispered. "I know you. I know very well- you're not going back to the workhouse. Be the smart you. Seize a chance. Stay safe." She paused." I'll miss you."

"Same," I said, pinning a smile to my face. "But we'll meet someday soon.

"But I didn't think we'd ever meet again."

Chapter 9

"Don't you start talking to me!" I yelled. "You lot are just evil! That's what you are."

"Well, what do you expect me to do? Just doing my job." Replied the taxi driver.

"Yes. But how do you think I feel - being taken away from my friend? We're not even meant to be at a workhouse at this age. You should bring forward this complaint to the police! You should..."

"Your imagination runs wild. We're talking in the twenty first century, not the Victorian times."

"Yeah? Well, you don't know what we do there, just because it doesn't look like a warehouse!" The taxi driver sighed, so I stayed silent. God, why was the journey so long- it's been more than two hours now.

"This does not look like London," I said, slowly taking my seatbelt off. "Where are you taking me?"

"Put your seatbelt on, for goodness' sake. I'm taking you back to the..."

"No, you not! The warehouse isn't that far away! Where are you taking me? Who do you think you are? Who do you think *I* am? Cause if you think you can trick me, you're wrong. *I* am no fool!"

"Look, if you stay silent, I'll tell you where I'm taking you. "The taxi driver said, as calm as ever." The calmness of his voice got my temper to the highest level. I couldn't control it any longer. "You idiot!" It came out before I could stop myself.

"I'm so sorry. I'll take that back. I really didn't mean to -it just came out and..."

"It's fine... I'm taking you to an orphanage." He replied whilst parking the car.

"Like you have the authority to do so." I retorted.

"Well, there's nothing you can do about it."

"Well, I know what an orphanage is if I see one. That is not an orphanage."

"Course not. It's where I'll book you into the orphanage session- you know-getting to know everyone, learning how it works there and other stuff," he replied, getting out of the car. "And you stay in the car." He said, and he locked the door. *I know very well you're not going back to the workhouse. Be the smart you. Seize a chance.* Maddie's words were playing in my head.

How did she know I wasn't going to the workhouse? *Seize a chance.* This was my chance. It was now or never. I tried pushing the door to my right. It wouldn't budge. I tried the door to my left. It wouldn't budge either. Passenger and driver's seat. Both wouldn't budge. I gave up-there was no point. That was until I saw the buttons underneath the windows on the driver's side. There were four. I pressed the first button. Nothing happened. Second button.

Nothing. Then I pressed the third one. *Click.* I opened the driver's door. It worked. I grabbed my bag with my money in it and ran.

The car started beeping louder and louder. I ran on and on and on until I couldn't hear the beeping. I leaned against a wall, trying to catch my breath.

Shouting was becoming louder behind me. I clutched my Side and ran on, quickening my pace, not daring to look back. I saw an alleyway and darted into it, hiding behind a bin. *Not the best of hiding places, but it will do.* I poked my head around to see the taxi driver running down the street. I breathed out and leaned my head back on the wall.

I was in such a state. My clothes. I could use my money to buy new ones. I edged down the alleyway before breaking into a run until I reached the end of it. There was a busy road, definitely not safe. I could easily get tracked down. Maybe running away from the orphanage wasn't such a good idea. I could've stayed there until I made my new escape plan and found somewhere to stay.

Or maybe I should just stay there permanently. I turned back, then stopped. I was screwed if I went back. If I came out of nowhere and then disappeared a few days later, they were bound to track me down. I turned and headed for the busy road.

The road to my left seemed to have fewer shops than the shops to my right, but if I went to the road to my right, it would lead me to the top of the street of the orphanage session thing.

I took the road to my left, putting my head down so I could not be recognised. I carried on walking, taking a right at the end of the street, then turning left. Right, left, right, left. After what seemed like hours, I reached a lane filled with shops.

That's when I realised how hungry I was. There were quite a few restaurants I went past, my stomach grumbling past each one. I hadn't eaten in a long time. I finally reached a lane and gave up, deciding to get to the first restaurant I saw. It smelt delicious.

A fish and chips shop, with a friendly-looking man at the shutter, a girl probably my age standing next to him. I guessed they were African.

She disappeared as I approached the shutter. I look so trampy. Well, I guess that was the definition of me-a 12-year-old girl who lost her friend and is alone in the world with nowhere to go. But then it was kind of my fault, thinking that escaping the warehouse was such a great idea. I thought it would run so smoothly. But then I never thought about where we would live. "Your order?" I looked up.

The man looked young to be serving, probably a few years older than me. "What do you give?"

"Just fish and chips." He smiled. "But they're extra tasty."

"I'll take one order then, please."

"Three pounds fifty then." I gave him the money. Was that expensive or cheap? I didn't know. I got the fish and chips wrapped in paper. I was going to ask why it was on paper but then thought the better of it. Just then, the girl's head popped up again. She smiled at me. I realised how alike they looked, especially when they smiled.

"Are you two siblings?"

"Yes," the girl said. She grinned. "I'm his older sister." The man rolled his eyes and smiled.

"Yeah, right."

"Why are you dressed up like that?" The girl asked. Oh god. How do I say it? When we I used to go to primary school, we had World book day.

"My school held a world book day contest. We had to dress up as...as anything."

She looked at me sideways and frowned. Did I say something wrong?

"The summer holidays began yesterday. How is your school still open?" The girl asked.

Ooops.

"Oh..." I said.

"I think we should leave her alone. She probably needs to go home or to... school now. "The man said.

"Oh, sorry," The girl said. "Where do you live? I've never seen kids come on their own."

"I...I...err...I." I sighed. "I don't know."

"I knew something was up. You seemed so reluctant to go. And you look such a mess. You're coming to my house. I'm sure I could find you something to wear."

She disappeared before I could protest. I got a look at the shutter. It looked so modern, so big. "Hi." I looked at her.

We were at similar heights. She was wearing white sliders, white jeans, a black top and a red and black chequered cardigan tied around her waist. She pulled my arm gently and led me to the back of the shutter. David was behind us, clearing up.

"Now, tell me everything. How can you not know where you live? That'll give me something to listen to."

"Why is your brother clearing up? Are you closing your shop now?"

"David's just clearing up the mess I made at the back."

"Ella, how on earth do you manage to make such a mess," David called.

"I was experimenting. It went a bit wrong. Then..." replied Ella. "Ok, ok. Let your friend talk." David cut in. I felt a surge of happiness. *Friend.*

"Well," Ella said, staring eagerly at me.

"Tell me."

"Well, I used to live in an orphanage,"

"You're an orphan. No way, I'm so sorry! "Ella cut in.

"It's fine," I replied. I talked about how fun the orphanage was, how we were dragged into the workhouse at nine and worked for miss Moss, all the torture we went through, and then we escaped. Maddy became sick. I was meant to be sent back to the workhouse.

The taxi driver drove all the way here to take me to another orphanage, but I ran out of the car and found my way here. I missed out the part about Matilda.

"So, you've escaped twice. You have nowhere to go." David said, who joined me halfway through.

"That's pretty much what it is. Gosh, telling my life story has made me realise how hectic my life has been so far," I exclaimed.

"So, you're telling me that taxi driver drove you from London to Southampton,"

Ella said. Southampton. Is that where I was? I nodded.

"Yep. He drove me all the way from London to here."

"Amber's coming in a bit. She's going to take me home whilst David stays at the shop. You're coming with me."

Ella said. "Oh, but..."

"No buts, you're coming with me, "Ella declared. "Ummm...thanks, but you don't mind, do you?" I asked. "Why would we? It would be nice having you to stay." David put in.

"Wouldn't your parents mind though?" I asked. I really liked the idea of going to stay with Ella and David. I felt like I could trust them. And they were genuinely pleasant. But I didn't want to be a burden on them either.

"Their abroad right now. Gonna comes in two weeks. But they won't mind, I'll tell you that."

"Well, ok. It's nice of you to do this for me," I paused.

"Thanks a lot."

Chapter 10

Amber was really pretty, presumably David's age. She had ocean blue eyes and long black wavy hair. She took us back to Ella's house, asking me about how I got to Southampton.

I summarised it as much as possible, and she seemed to be really interested in the workhouse part, so I exaggerated it a lot. We finally got to Ella's house. From what I saw so far in Southampton, the houses were pretty nice, but Ella's house was exquisite.

It stood big and tall and grand. The front garden had a circle of different flowers and a little water fountain in the middle, with one bird on either side of it. When we went inside, she took us into the vast living room, where I and Amber put our stuff. Whilst Amber started to cook something, Ella took me to her room.

"Here. Take this. The showers are just down the landing." She gave me a white dressing gown and white towel and a bottle of soap.

"I'll find you a few outfits. We'll see which you want."

I smiled gratefully and headed toward the shower room. It was just perfect. So far, the whole house had fluffy grey carpet.

The bathroom was huge. There was a single bath at the back, with two standing plants on either side. On the right was a long grey cupboard and two sinks on top of it. On the left was a wide glass shower, and next to it were *three* electric heaters. I came out in the super soft white dressing gown and the white towel wrapped around my head. I came out in the super soft white dressing gown and the white towel wrapped around my head. I went into Ella's room, holding my folded, hand-washed clothes.

"I wanted to pick out clothes I thought would suit you, but they all seem like they would suit you, so you can choose whatever outfit you like."

I smiled.

"Thanks." There was a wide variety of outfits, Different shirts and trousers, jeans, skirts and dresses. I chose a dress with a black top and a flower print skirt. Dresses haven't always been my favourite, but I didn't want to keep Ella waiting.

The dress fit perfectly. I let my hair out, free from the sharp pulls of the plaits I used to do. Thank god I wouldn't have to do them silly- plaits anymore. We made our way downstairs, our noses sniffing hungrily in the air. I still hadn't eaten my fish and chips, which were still on the dining table.

"Lasagne!" Said Amber as we reached the kitchen. "Gosh, you look wonderful, Aleena." Amber exclaimed.

"Thank you." I replied. I looked at her in her white and black dungarees and her black white Converse shoes. I was trying to decide. A hard decision. Chips or lasagne. I had been dying to eat it, but now I wasn't so sure. I wanted to eat them both but I didn't want to look fat. And if I decided to eat the fish and chips, Amber might think I didn't want to eat her lasagne. Luckily, Ella helped me make up my mind.

"Amber makes the best Lasagne ever. You *have* to try it."

Then she whispered in my ear.

"Don't eat your chips-I've got something planned for tonight. Save it for then." She winked. We sat at the dining table. The table was long and rectangular, with eight chairs. There was a flower in the middle of it.

There were two long windows with rose gold curtains. Next to it was a long black cabinet with a flower in the middle and a circular mirror on the wall above it.

It was true. Amber's lasagne was the best-not that I had ever tasted lasagne before. Amber wasn't eating. Instead, she was telling me her life story. "It's sad being an only child," She said. "But hearing that you don't even have a family makes me feel a lot more grateful for even *having* a family. I and David go to university together. We've known each other since Year three. We went to secondary as well. But..." The doorbell rang. "Must be David."

Said Amber excitedly. Why was *she* so excited?

Ella grinned. I knew what she was thinking. I grinned back.

Chapter 11

"What time is it?" I asked.

"Nine thirty-two," Ella replied.

"When does David close his shop?"

"Nine o'clock."

"So, I'm guessing David and Amber have dinner together," I said.

"Yeah." We were upstairs, and now I had time to appreciate her room. It had a double bed, grey carpet, a pink fluffy rug, a white cupboard and a bedside cabinet. She had a dressing table with a chair and a mirror, with lights around it.

Her windows had light purple curtains and a *TV* on the wall. I was so excited. Ella went for a shower, telling me to choose which pyjama's I wanted. She came back later, and I watched her comb her afro hair. I stared thoughtfully at her long, thick hair.

"Would you like me to do braids on you-I mean French braids?" She stopped midway in combing her hair.

"Can you actually do French braids?" I looked at her reflection in the mirror. She seemed impressed.

"Yeah. We always did it in the workhouse." I replied.

"Please do." She said. So, as I braided her hair, she told me stories of when she went to her parent's country, Ghana. She told me about the animals she saw. "Once, we were in a boat on a lake. I was quite little, around five or six. David was dragging his fingers over the lake, and a shark bit his fingers off. Mum and Dad took him to the hospital, and they grew back again." I looked at her, stunned.

" Are you *sure* his finger got bitten off?" I asked.

"Yes. David told me. I saw it with my own two eyes as well."

"If it got bitten off, I don't think it'll grow again."

"It will. I'm telling you. Just cause your fingers have never come off..."

"Ok then, let's do a little experiment. Cut your fingers off and we'll see if it grows back again."

"I'm good thank you," she replied. But she looked unsure. Gotcha. Now she knew fingers couldn't grow back.

"And are you sure there was a shark in a lake? It sounds very unlikely."

"Yes, now think about it- it doesn't sound very plausible." She replied. I finished her hair, and we both lay back in her bed and chose a movie to watch.

"I used to love this movie as a kid-I still do. I'm sure you'll love it too."

Lion king. The name itself sounded interesting.

"Wait, I'll be back - give me five minutes." Said Ella, and she swept out of the room. She was as good as her work and came back five minutes later. I held onto the remaining money I had left. What would I use it for? I didn't think I would have to buy new clothes. I felt really bad for wearing her clothes. It didn't feel right- It didn't feel right wearing her pyjamas. But Ella was insistent-like it was a command that *had* to be followed. She sat next to me. "Popcorn!" she exclaimed.

"And your fish and chips- I heated it up."

"Thanks!"

I exclaimed. "Let the movie night begin." Said Ella. And we dug in.

Chapter 12

The movie was great. I loved it. We were stuffed with popcorn by the end of it. David came in to say goodnight and told us he would take us shopping in the morning. I couldn't sleep.

The day was so hectic. We went to the hospital, and Maddy recovered, and I got taken away from her. The nurse's brother was meant to drive me to the workhouse but drove me over two hours away from London to Southampton.

I found my way to the fish and chips shop, and they received me into their home welcomingly. Why did they even do it? I was just a random stranger. All these thoughts occupied my mind until I fell asleep.

I woke up early in the morning.

Ugh. I guess was just so used to waking up really early. I looked at Ella, who was snoring *contentedly*. I sighed and lay back, squeezing my eyes shut. *This is the first time in a long, long time that I've been able to have a good sleep. Make the most of it.* My head was whirling, so I fell asleep.

"Wake up, lazy head. Anyone would have thought you hadn't slept in years."

"Sorry. Why do I feel so lazy? I was wide awake really early in the morning."

"Never mind that. David's taking us shopping in two hours. We'll get up now and make breakfast, shall we?"

"Sure." I got changed into the dress I wore yesterday. Ella got out a new outfit. We made our way downstairs. "I love fried eggs, potato waffles, beans and toast for breakfast," Ella said.

"I'm guessing you never had it at the workhouse?"

"Yeah. The last time I ate it was about five or six years ago in the orphanage."

"That's just messed up. How did you even *survive*? I would *not* be able to *cope*". David said. He definitely looked like he just woke up.

"It was hard. Especially since there was no way of escaping from it." I said, shuddering at the thought of miss Moss catching us escaping.

"Then how *did* you escape?" David and Ella asked in unison.

"There was an underground tunnel. It's usually locked. It was unlocked cause there was gonna be some work in there. We used this opportunity to get out of there, and my friend somehow found a route of getting out through the tunnel."
"Wow. That's smart. And cool. A real adventure."
"Yeah. It was. Kind of scary, though. I was at midnight, you see."
"It's like having a chat with somebody from the past. Past happening in the present. So, it's still going on, I guess?" David said.

"Yeah. All the other unfortunate kids there. I wish I could help them somehow-or for them to escape. But I can't try right now-its way, too risky..."

My voice tailed off. I had only known these people for a day and was already giving them so much information. "And breakfast is ready!" Declared Ella.

Just then, the doorbell rang.

"I'll get it." Said, David.

"Let's get the table ready. It's probably Amber." There were millions of cupboards. Which were the dishes?

"One to the right. Dishes cupboard." Said Ella, whizzing around the room.

"Hey!" said Amber. "Hi Aleena, how are you doing?"

"Good," I replied. I was too busy staring at her ears. *Three* piercings. Forget that- I didn't even have one.

And it looked really nice too. Gosh, it must've hurt. "Do you two *mind* if I steal David for the day?" Asked Amber.

I looked at her, baffled.

"What do you mean." I asked. She blinked, then gave a self-conscious laugh.

"No, we don't mind, Amber," Ella said.

"No, it's because I know David had planned to take you two shopping, but we have a job interview- for a learning experience-internship. But I guess David *forgot.*" David scratched the back of his head.

"Sorry guys. I wanted to be able to show you around Southampton a little, Aleena-so could get used to it."

"Oh, David-its fine- your internship thing is more important. What time is it at?" I asked.

"Uh...Ummm...well..." David started.

"Well...?" Amber asked.

"Uhhh...I dunno."

"Well, for *your* information, Mr Oblivious, it's at half ten today." Replied Amber. I giggled.

"Holy cow!" David exclaimed. "We better get a move on. Don't wanna be late, do you?"

David and Amber got up and headed for the door. From the corner of my eye, I saw Ella making a heart shape with her hands, and peering through it, clearly having the centre people David and Amber. When they left, I asked Ella. "We're home alone. What are we gonna do?"

"We'll wash the dishes- then I'll show you exactly what we'll do," Ella replied with a sly grin. Oh no. This did not look good to me. I'd seen that smile many times before- it never meant something good.

Chapter 13

"You're nuts!" I screamed. "What is David gonna say if he finds out what we're doing?"

"Who cares what he says? Were almost thirteen-almost teenagers. We can do whatever we want."

"Not whatever we want. Let's think this through," I said, stopping, hands on hips.

"You're showing me around most of Southampton *and* your taking me to your favourite restaurant *and* you're taking me to the beach and *then* you're taking me to see your cousin."

"Yeah. Doesn't it just sound like the perfect outing? It'll be so much fun."

"I have no doubt," I replied. "But at least tell David so he'll know where we're at. If anything happens, we can tell him. And besides, I highly doubt we'll get back to your house before he finishes his interview."

"Take a chill pill, girl," Ella said, exasperated. "It'll be fine. Trust me, I've got this under control."

And she winked. That didn't look or sound good to me either- that wink, I'd seen that one many times too. I sighed and followed Ella, taking in the town around me as she pointed out various shops and restaurants.

It struck me as shocking that I was going out, well, going on a tour with someone I knew for only two days. I couldn't help feeling there was something unpleasant waiting for me around the corner. Something that would make me regret it. Really badly. Right now, I had to keep my fingers crossed and start praying hard.

"And now we'll go to my favourite restaurant."

"Great." I smiled. It wasn't like I didn't like Ella, even though it might seem like it. She was a fun, high-spirited, kind, willing girl, but she was doing something risky, and much as I was trying to enjoy it, I couldn't. I would have enjoyed it a lot more if David was there-knowing that I didn't have to worry if anything happened. But that heart of mine wouldn't just stop beating so hard I could literally hear it thumping in my head. I took a deep breath.

"Look, thanks a lot for bringing me here. It means a lot, especially since this is one of the nicest things done for me in ages. I apologise for being so...such a spoilsport earlier."

"Tell me about it." She scoffed. "Now, look. Who's right?"

"*But,* we should head back to your house after this. I still don't think it was a good idea, despite how lovely today was —so far." She rolled her eyes.

"We're *not* going back-you're just not used to this kind of stuff. Trust me, by the end of today, you'll regret wanting to go back so soon."

"I dunno, if you say so," I replied, giving in.

"Don't worry, I'll take care of you, and if anything happens to you, I'll take the blame-not that anything *will* happen." I nodded and forced a smile.

"So, tell me about your school."

"I'm so excited I'm going to year eight after the summer holidays."

"Woah-isn't that like, such a big year?"

"Well, yeah, I guess, but trust me, compared to the older kids, you're a little nobody. But some of them are decent."

I stared at her, wide-eyed. "Yeah, but overall, it's not too bad, I would say, just that work gets harder. Before you know it, you're doing your GCSEs."

"Whoa, I don't know much about it-as in GCSEs, but I don't think I'll ever do it. I don't even know what I'm doing in my life."

"Did you not go to school before?"

"I did from nursery till year four, then I moved into the workhouse in the summer holidays-very unexpected."

"Would you like to be adopted into a family?"

"Yeah. I would, More than ever. I don't really know how to explain it-loads of people feel different. I don't exactly feel sad that I'm an orphan because you don't know what it feels like to have a loving family. I guess no other family can love you as much as your own one, but I dunno. But being in a family where I feel I will be loved is enough."

We ate the rest of our meals in silence, deep in our own thoughts. What was I doing? I couldn't stay in her house forever. I just hoped that somehow, something would happen where I could find a family where I belonged.

"Now, we go to the beach." Said Ella.

"I can't wait," I replied.

We went to the beach and splashed in the waves and sunbathed. We splashed about in the waves for a bit longer.

"Umm, don't you think we should go now?" I asked.

"Yeah, we should. I'll race you to the rocks."

"It's quite slippery..." I began, but she was off, so I ran after her. We made it to the slippery rocks through the water.

"I think you are right. These rocks are dodgy." Said Ella. "But I'll be careful." she said. She started running, higher and higher, and before I knew it, she slipped. Like that. She bashed her head on the rocks and started sliding down. I jumped out of the way and grabbed her arm, just in time to stop her from crashing her head on the sharp rock beneath her. I fell and scrambled towards her. I gasped. Her head had a large nasty cut and there was blood trickling down the side of her head. I brushed my wet hair from my face and looked for something to wrap her head with. Nothing. She was murmuring something.

"What?" I asked.

"My phone. Call David."

Of course.

I grabbed her phone that was lying next to her. I scrolled to her contacts. David. I called the number. "Hello. You need to come to the beach right now, David. It's an emergency."

"Ok, I'm on my way, but what the hell are you lot doing at the beach. What the hell are you doing out, as a matter of fact?"

"Long story, Ella hit her head against some slippery rocks- the one in the water. And her head's bleeding really bad."

"Call the ambulance."

"Got it." I ended the call and phoned the ambulance.

Chapter 14

"Her head is bleeding bad."

"Get her into the ambulance."

"Right."

"Don't worry, darling, you'll be fine."

All the paramedics were surrounding Ella, and David looked as if he might faint. We all got into the back of the ambulance and drove off to the hospital.

"What the hell was doing out? I am so dead by mum and dad." David said, head in hands.

"I'm sorry, David." Murmured Ella. "You know you shouldn't have gone with her." David started to say to me. I was speechless...I knew David would be mad. He only had every right to be. "David..."

"It wasn't her fault- it was mine-I didn't listen to her when she told me it wasn't a good idea." Ella slurred.

"And *at least*, you should have let me know." David continued.

"Look, I'm sorry, ok," Ella whispered. "And I'm sorry to you too, Aleena." I nodded, but that wasn't my focus.

My focus was something- someone I saw at the beach just before I entered the ambulance. I kept trying to convince myself that it wasn't that person I saw, but something in my heart convinced me that I saw *The Mayor*. But why would *he* be here? And the worst part was that *he* saw me! No, he couldn't be here. Why Southampton out of all places? I shook myself. *Think of something nice*. But right then, I couldn't think of *anything* nice. then, I couldn't think of *anything* nice.

We got to the hospital, and I waited in the waiting area. I was so scared Ella had gotten a concussion. But she came out about half an hour later with a bandage around her head.

"I'm alright." said Ella, her face bright again and her eyes no longer filled with pain. We headed back to Ella's house, and she went straight to bed.

There was a guy, waiting at the door. From the way David greeted him, I guessed it was a friend of his. He came in and I went to Ella's room.

"Feeling better," I asked.

"Yeah-they cleaned up my wound, then they put gel- which really stung, then they wrapped it. They told my parents and whatever too."

"What were your parent's reactions?" I asked.

"I don't know-they were just scared. Oh, by the way, they're coming next week. Remember when I called them and told them about you, well, they're so excited to see you. They asked about you today, and I told them how you saved me from getting killed."

"How did I save you from being killed?"

"Cause, *silly,* you grabbed my hand before I hit my head on the sharp rock-trust me- if not for you, I wouldn't be able to talk to you right now."

"Well, it was nothing. I'm glad I saved your life then." I smiled.

"It was definitely something. Thanks, if I haven't already said it."

"You're welcome."

Chapter 15

It was the day before Ella's parents were coming. Luckily, Ella's head was better and healed just in time. I was so nervous-what would they think of me?

Would they actually mind me being there? I was out with Ella and Amber, who I realised, was really a close family friend to them. She was looking more and more scared as time came. When it was time to go to Ella's place, she drove off in her own direction, so I and Ella walked back to her house.

What happened next was the most unexpected, the worst experience of my life, for then. As we walked to Ella's house, a police car was standing outside with none other than *The Mayor*, and his son.

"What's going on," I could hear Ella's trembling voice next to me.

"Uh..."

"Sneak to the back of the house." Whispered Ella. This has *got* to do with me. Why else would *The* Mayor be here? I couldn't tell Ella that, though. I just had to pray I didn't get caught and nothing goes wrong. David's shouts were coming from inside.

"She isn't here. Go away. Leave my house. No, she's not here."

They tracked me down. And there was me thinking the Mayors' son was nice.

"Who tracked you down? Who did you think was nice?" Ella asked. Oh no. *She heard me. It wasn't a thought.*

"What's wrong with you? It's not *a thought* 'cause I'm right next to you and you're saying stuff aloud."

"What's wrong with me? You're hearing my thoughts."

"I'm not hearing your thoughts, your speaking 'me' out loud," Ella shouted.

Gosh, why was she so mad?

The Mayor was taking David away. He had no right to. He wasn't even what he called himself. He was just some random guy in league with that witch of a Miss Moss. I didn't care at that moment. Even if I had to get taken back to the workhouse in exchange for David going free, I would do it.

He was out of the house, his hands tied behind his back. Ella was with him, screaming at the Mayor, who claimed to be the police. But his son was nowhere in sight. I marched up to The Mayor. "What are you doing?" I asked.

"Leave him alone. Answer me." I screamed, not knowing what had taken over me. My two plaits were whacking my face as I shouted. Those hands of mine were on the verge of doing something I would regret. "Go away, Aleena. You don't know what you're doing. Run away. Run!" David shouted.

What was he thinking-he seem more scared for me than he was for himself? I wasn't going to run. This was my *fault. It was because of me David was getting jailed. His* life was ruined cause of me. "Let David go, or I'll report you to the *real* police. Take me back to the workhouse if you want, and let him go."

"Your stupid, Aleena. You should go. Now. Run away. I mean it. Run." Said Ella.

"Get her. Don't let her escape, and this man's not going either." Said the Mayor, his voice calm and controlled. David's gaze was down. He stopped shouting and subsided. Ella looked like she was crying, and my heart was breaking into millions of pieces at that point. *The Mayor's* son was chasing me. My workhouse clothes were in my backpack, flapping on my back. I was not gonna let *The* Mayors son anywhere near me, so I legged it. I ran for my life. The road was so long. He was already gaining on me, begging me to stop. I tripped and fell and couldn't get up in time. He already knelt beside me. My hair all over my face.

"Are you ok?" He asked.

"Yeah." I replied. "Wait...what did you just ask me?"

He laughed. "You heard me the first time."

"Get away from me. Where your taking me to is illegal."

"I'm trying to help you." He said.

"Taking me back to the workhouse is not helping me - it's killing me."

"You don't understand. I'm helping you, as in I'm not taking you to that place of damnation."

I giggled. "That's a bit too dramatic - actually, I take that back. That's exactly what it is." Just then, Amber, her mum and another lady drove up to us. "Coming?" She smiled.

How is she being nice to me when I got her... David was practically arrested.

"You go with her. A family has been prepared to foster –well, take care of you, temporarily, until they get an actual family for you ready."

"And I'll also have a hard time explaining this to my father." He said dolefully. "You're telling him I'm getting fostered?" I asked, shocked.

"No. But I'll say you threatened to tell the police. He won't do anything to you then, I hope."

"Oh, thank you, thank you, thank you," I exclaimed.

"That's quite alright." He said. He got up and brushed himself down, and I got up too. I entered the car, but this time it was a different feeling. Not how it was when I entered the taxi, but a million feelings whirling inside me. If not because of Amber's friendly talks, funny jokes and interesting stories, I don't know *what* I would have done. I was heartbroken, except heartbroken wasn't a strong enough word. Sad-obviously. I wondered what Maddy was doing. But I was nervous and excited too.

This was just temporary, but it could be an opportunity to have a taste of having a family. Would I be an only child there? If not, is the child or children nice?... Throughout the two-and-a-half-hour journey, my mind continued whirling. I had gotten really close to her in the short space of time I'd been in Southampton-her and David. I'd ruined the lives of two innocent people whose parents were coming tomorrow. I couldn't ever forgive myself.

We got there, finally. Brighton was where this place was called. It looked like a nice area. We stopped outside the house. Nice house, but not as modern as Ella's and David's.

"Well," said the lady who drove me there. "Wish you all the best."

"Thanks," I replied. Amber came out of the car and enveloped me in a big hug. "It's such a shame that happened to David and his sister, but I hope everything gets better,

"But don't beat yourself up with it either. And stay safe. No running away-you seems to do that well." I laughed, I'll try not to run away."

"Good." She gave me a file of papers to give in when I went inside, and that somebody was coming in the morning to sign a contract with them. And she made her way back to her car.

Amber was young but caring. But then I guess you can be any age to be *that* caring and *show* that kind of love. The car drove off, with Amber waving in the window, and I walked up to the front door. Should I ring the doorbell, *or* should I knock. I decided to ring the doorbell. It was quite dark. What if they were asleep? The door opened, and the girl standing there welcomed me in.

"Follow me." She led me through the dark corridor, into a lit-up room. Nobody was there.

"I'll be having dinner with you if you don't mind. You must be hungry."

She said.

"Thanks, "I replied. We entered the room, and I shut the door behind me. She turned around, and I was shocked. "Maddy?"

Chapter 16

"Aleena!" She exclaimed. We ran and embraced in a hug. Gosh-It felt like we hadn't seen each other in like, forever, though, in reality, it had only been two or three weeks.

"What on earth are you doing here?" I asked.

"I could ask you the same question, but the answer would be that my family are taking care you. Gosh, I'm starving. Let's eat." So, we tucked into roast potatoes, gravy and green peas, carrot chips and Yorkshire pudding. It was delicious.

"We'll save our adventures tonight, though I'm still so shocked *you're* the person who got fostered. I just wish it was permanent."

"Oh, yeah."

"It would be so fun. You look lovely-how did you learn how to do those plaits?"

"Well," I said. "I think it would come under my adventures, so I'll save it."

"I still can't get over that fact that *you're* here right now. "She said.

"Can't wait, "I replied.

When we finished dinner, she took me into a room I guessed was her living room. Her whole *family* was there. I had an instant feeling of wanting to belong there. I wanted to be a part of their family forever. Two boys, around nine or ten, were playing table football in the corner of the room. The mum and dad were watching something on the telly and laughing.

Two girls were playing chess on the ground. Another girl was sitting on a couch, reading a book. *Six* kids. Plus, me, seven. I could quite understand now why they could only have me temporarily. They all looked up at me and smiled, and I suddenly felt really nervous.

"Ah, come in, come in." Their mum said. I came in, with Maddy beside me.

"Sorry, we couldn't give you a proper welcome." Said the dad.

"Oh, it's fine," I said. I could feel myself turning red. I guess I wasn't really good at composing myself as I thought.

"Maddy will take you to your room-in fact you will be sharing with her if you don't mind." She said, turning to Maddy.

"Oh no, I don't mind at all," I said.

"Then, Maddy dear, will you escort Aleena to your room?"

"Yes, mum."

So, we went upstairs. One of the boys stuck their tongue out at me as I walked out before they both started giggling. I stuck my tongue out and turned around quickly. "Those two boys have got cheek and nerve," I said to Maddy.

"Yeah. They're quite cheeky. If you get used to them, they're actually quite funny."

"Hmmm...if you say so."

We got to her room, and I was shocked. Her room was literally the same as Ella's.

"What? Disappointed." Maddy asked.

"It's lovely. Of course, I'm not disappointed." Maddy grinned and took me into the room.

"I don't get it," I said. "Why was I getting fostered so easy?"

"Well, it wasn't *exactly* fostering-it was just taking care of you until you get into a family of your own."

"Ah, that makes sense."

"So, let's choose which pyjamas you want to wear for tonight," Maddy said. There was a white and blue chequered top with matching trousers, so I chose that.

"So, tell me about your siblings," I said. Maddy's green eyes shone as I mentioned the word *siblings*.

"Well, the two boys- Brandon and James, are twins- they're ten - their birthday was three days ago. Then the two girls, Harmony and Rose, playing the board game are twins as well - they're both eleven. Then the girl who was reading the book-Ava is 14, two years older than us. "Wow, "I exclaimed.

"But I don't think you should be around Ava a lot," Maddy said.

"Why?"

"Because she hates me, and she's probably gonna hate you too."

"Don't worry-I'll master her. She won't hate me." "Hmmm. Ok. Do your magic." Maddy laughed.

Chapter 17

"Mum's calling you down." One of the girls said, standing at Maddie's door. I was guessing it was one of the twins. "Come, let's go." Said Maddy.

"Oh no, it's fine, Maddy. I'll take her down." The girl said. When we left Maddie's room, I said, "Thanks, Harmony, for taking me down."

She stopped in her tracks." How do you know my name, you creep?"

"Wild guess, I would say," I replied.

"Maddy told you, didn't she? "She said, grinning.

"She told me yours and your twins' names, so I guessed you were Harmony. You look like a Harmony."

She tossed her brown, wavy hair. "Thank you."

"So, which year are you in?" I asked her.

"Year eight- well I'm in year seven. I'm going into year eight after the holidays. Same as Maddy. My birthday is next week. I just have a late birthday."

"Well, I would be in the same year as you if I went to school."

"Are you a smart kid?" She asked.

"Well, would you count knowing your times tables smart?" She giggled.

"Yeah I guess so."

"Then I'm smart," I replied.

"It's such a shame your leaving at the end of the holiday. Your definitely much better company than..."

"Than?" I asked.

"No-one. It's fine." We got to the living room, where her mum was waiting. "Oh, hello." She said. I smiled politely. Oh, why did everybody have to stop what they were doing? Why did they have to stare?

"Please make yourself comfortable and at home here. I thought about getting you a little something, maybe, you could do it if you're bored or whatever. Let me just go get it."

"Your hairline's a joke." One of the boys said. Ugh.

That joke was just too lame. Too old for *me*. "Thanks. But you'll recognise the receding hairline you've got when you realise it takes longer and longer to wash your face each day."

There was a great commotion in the room. The boy turned red and started muttering to his twin. He better watches out. I wasn't going to go easy on him. Then he turned and I saw a name on his black hoody. James. "Where's your dad?" I asked.

"He's gone to work. He said to tell you he said goodnight. "Ava said.

"Oh...uh...ok..." I didn't know what to say. I realised that Ava wasn't reading a book, but in fact, was texting someone on her phone. I bit my lip.

How did I not realise that earlier on? I was gonna expose her, but then thought the better of it. *I'll stay on her good side. For now.* But I couldn't resist. *I'll half expose her.* Their mum came back with a bag, filled with a colouring book and hundreds of felt tips, colouring pencils and colouring books. Oh. I wasn't the type for drawing and colouring at all. "Thank you. This is so cute." I said, as politely as I could. I wondered what Maddy was doing upstairs. Ava was smirking at my awkwardness. *Maybe I wouldn't stay on her good side. For now.* "I like that phone cover. " I said, arms crossed.

She glared at me.

"Ava! Deceiving me like that. I told you, you were not allowed to touch your phone until you finished that unit in your textbook."

"But..."

"No buts." Said her mum. She was clearly trying not to shout. Then she turned to me. "Since you staying here temporarily, it would probably be a bit weird for you to call me mum, so, you could call me Marie, if you like."

"Thank you." I said. "I'll call you Marie then." She smiled, then turned to everyone else.

"Bedtime now. Upstairs whilst I get you all some hot chocolate." Hot chocolate before bed. That was amazing. "Come with us, Aleena." Said Harmony. "We'll give you a quick tour of the house."

"Nope. That will be tomorrow." Called Marie from the kitchen.

"Fine, we'll show you our room." Said Rose. I guess you could tell the difference between the two. Rose had grey eyes whereas Harmony had green. I followed them upstairs to their room. It looked just like Maddie's, but they had wallpaper. Spectrum wallpaper. "Your room is so cool," I said, fascinated.

"I know."Said Rose.

"Thanks." Said, Harmony. "You should go back to your room before mum comes with the hot chocolate."

"Ok, bye," I said. I left their room. And right there, standing on the stairs leading to the third floor, was Brandon. I guessed it was him because he had green eyes, whereas James had grey eyes. "Hey, new girl. "He said sleepily. He better not cheek with me, or he wouldn't have it easy. But he seemed calmer than James.

"Hey, *Brandon*," I replied.

"Well, you mastered our names fast." He marvelled. I tossed my head. "What can I say." He grinned.

"James uses the hairline joke way too much. It's actually kind of cringy. But nobody's ever given him an answer as funny as yours."

"Again, what can I say." I grinned.

"Were gonna have fun with you around. Too bad it's temporarily."

"Don't miss me too much when I go then."

"Brandon, Bed." he turned and fled up the stairs, pausing to wink at me and then heading off. I entered Maddie's room. She was sitting on her bed, writing something. "What are you writing?" I asked.

"Huh...oh...well...promise you won't think this is childish or silly or anything." She said.

"Promise," I replied.

"I'm writing a diary, ever since I came here. I write it every night."

"That's not silly, "I said. "I thought you were doing something like drawing a tattoo and planning to slick it on your arm."

"I was planning to do that. "Said Maddy, looking hurt. I gaped at her.

"I'm just joking, silly. Come. Let's begin the stories of our adventures."

"Hot chocolate! "Said Marie. She came with five mugs on a tray. "Help yourselves." We took our hot chocolate and said our goodnights before Marie left the room.

"So, you first, Aleena. Tell me what you've been up to. Yours is bound to be way crazier." Said Maddy.

"Ok...does anyone know that we know each other?" I asked.

"I don't think so. I never knew who it was gonna be myself. Mum just said a girl was gonna be staying for the summer holidays, blah blah blah. And when we asked for the name, she said: 'oh, you'll see'."

"Does it feel weird calling her mum?" I asked.

"No. It was awkward at first, but now I'm used to it."

"So, you're the only adopted child here?"

"Yep.When you left the hospital, I was in tears. I was begging them not to take me back. And then they asked me why I was so worried about going back when there was a family about to foster me. And I was surprised – I was like, how? Then they explained that my mum's sister was meant to take care of me but she knew she couldn't, so she sent me to the orphanage and was finding a family to foster me in the meantime.

"Really, I was meant to be adopted last year. I don't really understand what happened after that. It was just a series of me signing sheets and all that boring stuff, same with my parents. Then after that, I was taken to their home. That's pretty much it."

"Woah, that was long," I said.

"Will you ever visit your aunty?"

"Maybe. But I don't want to bother my parents- having to drive all the way to Cornwall. And besides, she's dealing with someone I don't want to deal with."

"Who? "I asked.

"Matilda."

Chapter 18

"Well, new girl. Happy you got me into trouble?" Ava was there, standing at the open door. "Happy to help." I winked at Maddy. "Ugh. Stop playing up. It's your first day here." said Ava, a mischievous twinkle in her eye.

"Don't be such a baby. You didn't even get in trouble. A mere telling off, I would call it. Surely a fourteen-year-old could get over it." I said. She grinned.

"How do you know how old I am?"

Maddy gave me a sharp nudge.

"You look fourteen. How else would I know?" I said. Hopefully, this would take me out of her bad books. She laughed.

"You're sweet. I don't think anyone's ever said I look my age. "I grinned. She didn't look her age at all. She was almost fifteen, but she looked like an eleven-year old-she was the same height as me.

"Teach me how to do those plaits." She begged. The two plaits that Ella called cornrows. Ella did in my hair came off, so I redid them whilst Maddy was telling her story. "Teach me as well!"

"And me too." Harmony and Rose were at the door as well. "Can we come in?" Asked Harmony.

"Yes, come in." Said Maddy. I could hear a slight irritation in her voice. I hoped she wasn't annoyed at everyone coming to talk to me. They all came in, and we all sat on Maddie's bed.

"Tell us, Aleena. How did you come to be here? Tell us, from the beginning, if you don't mind." Said Rose.

"Can we join too?" Said, James, standing at the door with Brandon.

"No, this is only girls' talk." Said Ava.

"But we want to know your crazy journeys too." Said, James. Why was *he* so interested? For all I know, he was probably gonna make fun of me the whole way. "Ok then." I said. "No cheek from you though - no noise either."

"Ok, Ok. I'm not a baby, you know."

"Oh, sorry, I didn't know that. Now come in." I said. Brandon had a smirk on his face. He better not be planning something too. "No cheek from you either, Brandon."

"Ok, your highness." He said. I rolled my eyes. Once they were all in, I began my story, all the way the beginning. From the orphanage to the workhouse, make sure to include Maddy so she wasn't left out. Maddy added her own stuff in, especially the part about Matilda. Then I told the part about escaping all the way to the end.

"That's so cool. And you didn't make anything up?" Asked James.

"Yep. Complete truth, from beginning till end. "I replied. "You work in a workhouse? I thought it only happened in the olden days." Said Ava.

"Yeah. It doesn't still happen. I think it's just this one case." Said Maddy.

Ava rolled her eyes at her.

"You're so evil. Poor David." Said Brandon.

"Yeah, I guess you could say I am," I replied.

"Amber's so sweet." Said, Harmony.

"Yep. One hundred percent agreeable." I replied.

Rose said: "Poor Ella, what's going to happen to her?"

"I don't know." I replied. "I hope David gets out of prison and she can live happily with her family."

"We should go to bed now. Aleena, you're probably tired after the journey here. Just before I go, it's good to have you here." Said Ava.

"Thanks Ava. And yes, I think we should all go to bed now." I said.

Everyone left.

"Well, how's your first day here?" Maddy asked.

"Great. I actually really like it here. I thought it would be hectic since there's so many kids here!" I replied.

"Oh, you just wait till tomorrow. You'll see what it's really like."

"Well, goodnight Maddy," I said.

"Goodnight, Aleena." She replied. And before I knew it, I could hear a gentle snore from her, which reminded me so much of the workhouse.

Chapter 19

"Wake up, sleepy head. Welcome to your first day at the Burton house!" Everyone was going crazy and was all surrounding me.

"Pick out your new outfit for today!"

"Come. We'll give you a tour of the house afterwards." "We'll go out later on our bikes. You'll come with us." "We'll go with a picnic."

"You can have anything for breakfast." Everyone was shouting so I decided to get up.

"Well then, we'll pick out my outfit for my first day at Burton's house," I said. There was a great commotion. "What's the noise!" Called Marie.

"Don't take too long, or your pancakes will go cold!" Pancakes! I remembered Amber's pancakes. Her mum helped me make my own too, and it was the best with honey. Harmony let out an excited squeal.

"Sorry, pancakes come first." Said Rose. She and Harmony rushed downstairs. "Don't worry, Aleena. I won't leave you. I'll help you pick out an outfit."

"Great! thanks." I replied, jumping out of bed. I headed to my cupboard and then stopped. "Maddy, are you gonna come?" I asked. She looked at Ava, then back at me. "Umm...no. I'm gonna join Rose and Harmony downstairs if you don't mind."

"It." I picked out an outfit which was matching with Ava's, at her request.

"Great. We're gonna look so Alike. We both got green eyes and brown hair. If only my hair was a rich brown colour like yours." Ava said.

"I think your brown her is very pretty," I said to her. She laughed-and at that instant I realised she was somebody who loved to be complimented.

"You know, to make us look really alike, we should both have the same hairstyle- you know, you could do those braids on me and you, then we'd look so similar," Ava said eagerly.

"Ok. I'll do mine first, so you can watch me do it, then I'll do yours."

At the end of it, we were almost identical. Almost. Her skin was paler as I was more tanned. I looked at us both in the mirror. We were both wearing pastel green cotton trousers with a white top and a long white cardigan.

"If your ears were pierced, I would have bought you earrings similar to mine. "Said Ava. I smiled at her.

"We should go down now."

"Yeah. I'm starving."

We got downstairs and everyone-apart from the boys and Maddy were still waiting.

"You took ages. We were waiting for you." Said Rose.

"Maddy, do you want to play basketball outside with us?" Asked Brandon. She jumped out of her chair and replied in the affirmative. Was she ok? She seemed really distant all of a sudden. I decided to ask her later.

"These are the best pancakes I've ever had," I said. Really, I couldn't pick between Ambers mum and this one. They were both very nice.

"Yeah, mum makes the best pancakes." Said Rose. "Hello. I'm back!" Said Justin.

"Dad!" Shouted Rose, Harmony and Ava at once.

"Hello, guys." Said Justin. "I just got..." He began before slipping.

"Dad! You should tie your shoelaces." Said Rose, trying not to laugh.

"Yeah. I know. But I was just too excited to see my princesses that I forgot!" He said. Justin got up and went upstairs.

"How are you so confident, Aleena- I mean, you're so self-confident. But if I were you, I don't think I would have uttered a word by now." Said Rose.

I smiled.

"I wouldn't call myself *confident*-you should have seen me when I met your parents. I was shaking to the knees!"
"You're so modest." Said Ava.

"Is being confident a good thing?" I asked her, confused. "Yeah…sometimes." Said Harmony.

"Now that was all done eating breakfast, let's give Aleena a tour around our house." Said Rose. They showed me the kitchen, living room, playroom, bedrooms, bathrooms, garage and garden. The whole house was amazing -it was almost like a mansion.

"I'm gonna speak to Maddy," I told them after the tour. When they showed me the garden, Maddy hadn't even bothered to look at me. I went to the garden and bumped into Brandon.

"Oops, sorry." I said. "Do you know where Maddy is? I need to talk to her."

"I need to talk to you." Said Brandon.

"But *I* need to talk to Maddy."
"Well, *I* need to talk to you *about* Maddy." I stopped.
"Go on then."
"Well, she was acting really weird. When my sisters said we should wait for you, Maddy didn't want to, and just ate her breakfast, like me and my brother. I asked her to come outside and play basketball to ask her why she did it-I mean, she *could* have breakfast if she wants to, it's just that, seeing as she hasn't seen you in a long time, I thought her behaviour was rather odd."
"Yes, it is." I said, deep in thought. "I'll go talk to her. Thanks, little one."
"Oy! I'm not little!"
"You are to me."
"Thanks a lot." He replied. I grinned.

"wait." I called out.

"What did she say to you?"

"I'm little and my little brain can't remember, right?" He replied.

"Little people don't always have little brains." I paused, I'm sorry. I promise I won't call you *little* again. Now tell me."

"Well, she said something about my sister, about..." "Ava! I knew it. thanks!" I exclaimed. Brandon rolled his eyes and went inside. I walked around the garden to the other side, where the pool was.

"Maddy?"

She was sitting at the edge of the pool, her feet dangling above the water. I approached her and sat next to her.

"Are you okay?" I asked. "We're riding bikes out in a few minutes. Come."

"I'm not gonna come. I might just stay and help mum cook supper. "Mumbled Maddy.

"Don't be ridiculous. Of course, you're coming." I looked at her.

"Why won't you come? You're not being yourself either. Where's the old Maddy gone?" She gave a tight smile.

"The old Maddie's still here."

"Tell me then, how come you're so upset." She looked away.

"I'm fine." I sighed.

"It's cause of Ava, isn't it? It's causes I'm hanging out with Ava." Her eyes went big.

"I told you to stay away from her. She's no good." "Well, I think she is good. She's been nothing but kind to me the whole day. Don't let her ruin our friendship." She gasped at my sharp tone.

"Well, our friendship won't last if you carry on hanging out with her." And she stood up and walked off.

"Maddy, wait, "I called, but she walked off. I decided
to go back inside. And who was there when I rounded the
corner other than *James*?

"You girls are so petty. Chillax. "And I pushed past
him. "Silly people. "I muttered.

"Who are you referring to as silly-me or Maddy?"
"Both," I replied.

"I'm off to tell Maddy then."

"No." I said. "Please don't."

"Then your gonna have to do something for me." he
said with a sly grin.

Oh boy.

Chapter 20

"It's not funny!" I shouted, half angry, half laughing. Rose, Harmony, Ava and Brandon were surrounding me, watching me going through the torture of giving James a foot massage.

"You give great foot massages for such dainty hands."

James sad and the others roared. For exaggeration, I put a peg on my nose, but now it was starting to hurt.

"Aw, you realised my feet smell just too nice, didn't you? "Said, James.

Ugh. All of this just so he doesn't snitch.

"That's it. I'm done with your *manky* feet." I said. "Nope. Or else you know what happens." Said James in a mocking voice. I could feel my face reddening.

"Your gonna explode." Said James, making a terrified face.

"So, your pardoned."

I didn't know how to react, whether to really explode or to laugh, so I just collapsed on the chair.

"Ava, come and take the picnic, so you lot can go out with your bicycles. Make sure you show Aleena which bike is hers."

Called Marie. Ava left to get the picnic.

"I think I'm gonna need to wash my hands with bleach," I whispered.

"Your pretty hands will go diseased." James whispered back.

"And besides, your hands are blessed now that you've touched my feet."

I grinned. "I would smack you if I wasn't against animal abuse." He gaped, as I walked off with Harmony and Rose following me.

"Be careful of her," I heard Brandon say. "She's a feisty one." We headed outside to the garage with Justin, who opened it up for us with his keys. Ava passed me a bike. "Sorry Aleena, but your bike is a boy bike. Do you mind?"

"No. Not at all."

In fact, I was delighted. I was worried I would have a bright pink bike or something Alike. Anyways, the bike was actually really nice, black, with orange stripes. "Do you know how to ride a bike?" Brandon asked me. "Not to be rude, just asking."

"For your information, I can ride a bike better than you can." I replied.

"Yeah, right. I brought the first aid kit for you cause you're gonna need it before we even cycle two yards."

He said slyly. "You'll be the one needing the first aid kit if you say another word." I replied.

"Yeah and you'll be sorry." Said Maddy from behind me.

"Ooo…two feisty fella's. Who knew *you* were so snappy, Maddy? I thought We were very sweet. Oh yes, I heard you say that to Aleena yesterday." I rolled my eyes and smiled at Maddy. "Let's go, guys." Called Ava. So were all riding off in a line to the park. I stayed in the middle, on the insistence of Brandon- 'Just in case, I hurt myself. I gave up trying to persuade him and challenged him to a race in the park.

"There's no way your gonna win, Aleena. Why bother?" Said, James.

"Stop being so rude." Said Harmony.

"I know, right? Leave her alone." Said Rose.

"Sorry I was just stating facts," James said.

"Fine. I'll race you *and* Brandon. We'll see who the loser is." I replied. I knew I would win anyways, so I had another plan in mind. To see if there was really another side to the boys.

Chapter 21

"Be careful, okay." Said Ava, taking my arm.

"Don't hurt yourself." said Maddy from my other side."

 "Well, I don't think hurting myself can be prevented, but it's worth it." I told all the girls my plan.

"That's so cool. I can't wait to see you do it."

"I wish I had thought of that." Said Rose, grinning. Ava walked out to the front, where me, Brandon and James had our bikes lined up. "Well, here we have Bummer Brandon, James the Jerk, and..."

"Miserable Aleena." Said James and Brandon, before high-fiving each other. I rolled my eyes. "Now let's begin." All the girls chanted, "THREE, TWO, ONE!" and we were off. I was in the lead Brandon behind me, and James just behind him.

"What did I say?" I called out.

"Maybe I'll give you a boost!" And I slowed down. Then, just as I was in line with them, I jerked my bike up and fell off. *This had to work. This had to work.* I lay as still as I could- practically motionless, eyes closed, lips pressed firmly together so that no laugh could escape. I could hear bikes falling. *Check.* Running towards me. *Check.* Kneeling down next to me. *Check.* "She's dead, thank god. We've gotten rid of her."

"No, she's actually not okay. Oy! She's passed out." "You lot can take care of her." Called back the girls. Perfect.

"No... I hope she's not hurt."

"Don't be daft."

 "CPR then."

"You're not crying, are you?" I opened my eyes. Don't cry for me. I'm Alive. Who knew you two cared so much." I said.

"No one here is crying. "Said, James.

"Then why are you wiping your eyes."

"It's... It's the sun."

"If you say so," I replied. I got up, but Brandon pulled me back down. "What was the point of that?" He asked. "Just an experiment." I replied, getting up again and pulling them both up as well.

"I'll try not to prank you like that again." I said, and walked up to the girls.

"Did you hear them?" I asked.

"Yeah."

"It was hilarious."

"I was literally crying out of laughter."

"Let's have our picnic, then we'll chill, then go back home." Said Ava, as she lay the picnic blanket.

"Gosh, it's so hot." Said, Maddy.

"I agree," I replied. I tried to stay on the good side so that at night time when it was just the two of us, I could have a talk with her. To be honest, it was all very confusing.

"Yeah," Said Harmony.

"Thank god mum packed some ginger beer in it." Ginger beer. *Beer.* "I don't drink beer," I said. They all laughed, including Maddy.

"What's so funny?" I demanded. "Ginger beer isn't *actually* beer," Maddy explained. It's a drink-a really tasty drink."

"Oh," I replied, turning red. "I knew you were stupid, but I never knew you were *that* stupid." Said James. "Alright, teasing has its limits." Said Brandon to James. "Let's tuck in!"

There were watermelon slices, grapes, strawberries, sponge cake, sandwiches and ginger beer. "I'm stuffed!" Said Ava. "We'd better get riding back home."

"Can we stay a little longer? A quick round of tag." Asked Harmony. "Oh, Harmony! We'll play it *our* special way." Said Rose to Harmony. Harmony agreed happily.

"Okay fine. Who's IT?" Asked Ava. And so, we played it-all seven of us. That's when I realised how supple everyone was. Then we had to play Harmony and Roses version-whoever's IT had to hop on one leg. We headed home in time for supper. I had been observing Maddy and Ava and the hostile glances at each other were enough to make me shudder. But I still didn't know why they hated each other so much. I would have to do something I would probably regret doing. But it would be worth it if I found out what it was and sorted it out.

Chapter 22

The day of the big outing came. We were to go to a massive funfair just outside of the city. I was so excited. I had been to a few funfairs when I was at the orphanage, so this would remind me and Maddy of those times.
Two weeks had gone past and the hostility grew more and more intense between Maddy and Ava. And I was quite sure on occasions they would almost fight to be in my company. James and Brandon said I should be feeling pumped, but really it made me feel really uncomfortable, so the only people I could talk about it too were Harmony and Ava. But today would be the day to discover why it was all happening. I was especially confused by Ava's behaviour.

Was she bothered with me was, like, a whole two years younger than her? But then I realised soon enough it was to make Maddy jealous. All this jealously was just stupid, I thought. We all headed to the funfair. We drove in a minivan- Justin driving in the front, Maddy, Marie and Ava just behind, me in the middle of Harmony and Rose, with James and Brandon at the back. We reached it in forty-five minutes.

It was just like I remembered. Merry go rounds, helter-skelter, Ferris wheels, funhouse, carousel, waltzed, bumper cars, the jumping jacks ride, Star flyer and the teacup ride. I looked around excitedly. Harmony and Rose were already running to the Star flyer and dragged me along, with everyone following behind. We sat in pairs, both sets of twins sat together, me and Maddy, Ava and Marie. and screamed.

The whole thing was a blur for me. It went so fast, we were all screaming our heads off. No one wanted to go on the Merry go round ride or the carousel, so we went to the

Halter shelter. I grinned to myself as I remembered Marie-
that was the first time I'd seen her so crazy.

We went to the helter-skelter, Ava trying to stay by my
side. That ride was amazing too. "I remember going on
this once." Maddy said, suddenly next to me.

"Yeah. That was so fun. You know, as much fun as I'm
having, I'm not finding it fun to my full heart's content."
"What a mouthful," Said Maddy. "What do you mean?"
"It doesn't feel right to be having fun when I know Ella
and David are facing the complete opposite. I'm gonna be
stuck with this guilt for the rest of my life."

"Remember what you said Amber said to you: Don't
beat yourself up with it and have fun-look, everyone's
going to the Ferris wheel. Let's go." I didn't even have to
turn around to feel the hostile looks from Ava behind me.
It was like it was piercing through me. Maddy seemed to
sense it too. "Aleena, please do something about it." Said
Maddy. "About what?" I asked. "About Ava," She hissed.
"I'm meant to live with her - I hate being on her bad side
all the time. "I will," I said, then I looked her in the eye.

"I promise."

"So, what's this plan of yours." She asked.

"I'm not telling you, but you're gonna have to play
along."

That was all I said, and we rushed to the Ferris wheel.
After visiting all the rides, we wanted to go on, we went to
the restaurant where I ordered fish and chips. That was the
last big outing I was going to have before going to my new
foster family-that was in two weeks. I was going to meet
them next week, though, for the filling of sheets and all of
that stuff.

We returned home after that and I started my plan for
Maddy and Ava. I let Rose and Harmony into my plan.
Since Ava loved compliments and graciously returned
them, our plan was to give compliments from Maddy Ava-

except Maddy never said it. And the plan would have to start the next day.

Chapter 23

"Woah...Maddy was right. You look stunning in that dress."

She was wearing a bright pink dress which hurt my eyes and a black denim jacket. Definitely not my type. She did that laugh that annoyed me so much.

"Oh, thank you." She said, tucking her hair behind her ears and making her eyes as big as saucers. Then she stopped her acting. "Did you say? Maddy... Maddy said I looked nice?"

"Yep. Is that so hard to believe?" I replied. "Oh...no. Not at all. Umm...well, she looks nice as well in her lilac dress too."

"Yeah, I agree... I'll go tell her now that you said that," I said.

"Wait...no...I..." She began, but I ran before she could finish her sentence. I went to the next room where Rose was. She high-fived me and we went to Maddy, who was with Harmony.

"You won't believe what Ava said about you!" I said. "She said you look nice in your dress." Rose continued. Listening to it, I realised how stupid it sounded. Still, it was a big thing for Ava to say about Maddy. Maddy crossed her arms.

"What did you tell her?" She said. "I knew she would guess that I did that. "I said that you said that she looks nice today," I said. Maddy turned pink. "I don't think I like her pink dress, but at least she thinks I didn't tell you to tell her she looks nice. "

That wouldn't give it away. "Cool. Step one complete." Said Harmony. "Girls, It's lunchtime!" Called Justin. "Plan two will happen after Lunch." I declared.

"It is stupid and make me look like a wimp." Maddy groaned.

"Don't worry," Said Rose. "Yep. We've got it all under control." Added Harmony, Winking at Rose. After lunch, we went to the garden to play volleyball. We dragged James and Brandon into it, promising to do their Chores for the day. All they had to do was to play volleyball against Ava and Maddy. Meaning Maddy and Ava would have to work together. Me, Harmony and Rose chilled by the swimming pool and watched them.

"I can't believe you're leaving us in a week and a half." Said Rose.

"Yeah, next week, she'll be seeing her new foster family." Said Harmony. "I know, but let's not think of that now. We'll make the most of the time I've got left with you." I replied. I genuinely didn't like thinking about leaving this family.

Although Marie and Justin were "temporary parents", they treated me like their own daughter and were like parents to me. Anyways, I couldn't think of *that* when I had to watch the intense battle between the boys and the girls. They made a great pair and worked perfectly together. It was as if they were never enemies.

It was nice to finally see them laugh together. Just as the game was ending, we rushed inside to give Ava and Maddy time, also to take over James and Brandon's table football. The finale would be at bedtime. were never enemies. It was nice to finally see them laugh together. Just as the game was ending, we rushed inside to give Ava and Maddy time, also to take over James and Brandon's table football. The finale would be at bedtime.

"I know, but let's not think of that now. We'll make the most of the time I've got left with you." I replied. I genuinely just didn't like thinking about leaving this family. Although Marie and Justin were "temporary parents, they treated me like their own daughter and were like parents to me. Anyways, I couldn't think of that when I had to watch the intense battle between the boys and the girls.

They made a great pair and worked perfectly together. It was as if they were never enemies. It was nice to finally see them laugh together. Just as the game was ending, we rushed inside to give Ava and Maddy time, also to take over James and Brandon's table football. The finale would be at bedtime. "You need it anyway, Aleena," Said Rose. "This could be the last time we have this."

"Yeah. Shh-they 're coming."

Later on, that night, Ava, Maddy, Harmony, Rose and me were munching on muffins, watermelons, biscuits and chocolate chip cookies. But this was where the plan came in.

The cookie packet had five cookies in it, but I hid one. The last cookie would be between Maddy and Ava. Then we would see what would happen. Knowing how smart Maddy was, I was afraid she would point out she knew we were hiding the last cookie or start demanding for it. But luckily, she didn't. She seemed way too busy wondering whether to do something about the last cookie. After a long awkward silence, Ava said. "You can have the cookie, Maddy. It's the last one."

"Oh no, it's fine. You can have it." Replied Maddy. There was silence.

"Just take it. I don't want it anyways." said Maddy. "O... Ok...thank you." Said Ava, taking the cookie. "Well, kindness always pays off. There's another cookie here." said Harmony, passing the cookie to Maddy. "Oh, thanks." Maddy said and the way she ate her cookie showed how much she really wanted that cookie. "So, I thought I might just bring this up now," I began. I could feel Maddy tense next to me, and Ava, holding her breath. "Ava, I don't mean to jump to conclusions or anything, but...why do...

why do you dislike Maddy so much." I was going to say hate, but it sounded too harsh.

"Well...I... It's hard to say." Said Ava.

"We're your sisters. You can tell us anything." Said Rose. "Well, I just didn't know how to react when..."

"Don't hesitate." Said Harmony.

"Oh my gosh, this is so embarrassing. I just realised how stupid I was. And I'm so much older than you timid things." She said, trying to smile.

"well. "I frowned, crossing my arms.

"Just joking," Replied Avalos. I'm sorry, Maddy. I've got a lot to apologise about, but why I hated you so much, I just can't bring myself to tell you why I despised you so much."

"Well, that was brave of you," Maddy sneered. She rolled her eyes. "And the first thing I want to apologise to you about is your diary journal thing. I only said it was silly cause I wanted you to feel bad."

"Second step completed," I said.

"Well, in all our twin years, we've never seen Ava admit she was wrong." Said Harmony to Rose, who nodded her head vigorously in agreement.

"Well, I'm sorry, but I guess I will have to tell Maddy why you were like that to her," I said.

"You know?" Asked Ava, bewildered.

"Yes...well, partially. You see, I may have taken a tiny peek at Maddie's journal..."

"Why did you read it?" Maddy hissed, suddenly filled with fury. I knew I would regret it. I looked down guiltily. "I'm sorry, but I thought...please don't be mad."

"We'll see if it's worth it." said Maddy, turning her back to me.

"Well, let's make this quick. I'm stuffed *and* I'm really tired." Said Harmony.

"Ok. I'll say it and then we all have to go to bed. I thought you hated me when you first came, so I thought I'd hate you back. And since your second oldest, mum and dad were acting like you were the oldest, giving you *my* big sister responsibilities, and...and I thought they were just trying to replace me because I wasn't good enough. I know it doesn't make sense. I'm sorry." And with that, she got up and left.

"Well, that's sorted. Poor Ava. I'm gonna go to sleep. Let's go, Harmony."

"Bye, guys. See you tomorrow." Harmony whispered. As soon as they all went to their rooms, I heard footsteps. I lay down and squeezed my eyes shut. Room by room, Justin came and stood outside each one, listening for noise. Satisfied there was no noise, he went back upstairs. From the loud thump, I knew he tripped on the stairs. I could imagine him looking around to see if anyone saw him trip, like he always did when something embarrassing happened to him. I bit my lip to stop myself from laughing.

"Well, Maddy, all is well now," I said.

"Yeah. And I'm not mad at you," She said.

"Just...don't do it again." I could hear the smile in her words. "Goodnight." I said. "G'night." she replied sleepily. And in seconds, she was fast asleep.

Chapter 24

I was so nervous. The time had finally come for me to visit my foster family. "Have a good time. "Said Justin. His words normally never made situations better, and it certainly didn't help this time either. I looked at him blankly.

"They're here!" Shouted everyone. They were all sitting on the window sill, watching out for them. "Justin, I don't think I can go now. My legs are so shaky. I think they might have to drag me with them."

"It'll be fine. "Said Justin, laughing. "Enjoy your outing." The doorbell rang. I turned around to all the grinning faces and gave a quick shaky wave, then opened the door. "Hello there, sweetheart. How are you?" A pretty lady stood at the door, a scarf around her head. She was a Muslim? Well, she would have to teach me everything she knew. "I'm fine, thank you."

"We are a big Family you know," She said, walking down the steps beside me. I could see her bright, white, shining teeth as she spoke. She smelt of jasmine scent- Ava's favourite perfume scent. "You'll see them all, in the minivan." I wanted her to know I was like her, that I was a Muslim as well, but I didn't know how to put it. "Will you teach me about Muslims one day?" I asked. She stopped and looked at me. "Why? I mean I would, but why do you want to know?"

"You didn't know? They didn't tell you? I'm a Muslim myself." I said. "Yeah I knew that, *obviously*." She replied hastily. The was an awkward silence until we reached the car. Why did I say that? Obviously, she would've known. This was one of the times where I just wanted to punch myself for not staying quiet at the right time. She opened the door and I went into the back seat, next to a little girl. I was so uncomfortable. I was so nervous I wanted to run back into the house and not go with them. But what choice did I have? "So," said the man driving the van. I guessed he was the man of the house.

"We're looking forward to getting to know you properly. We're going to take you to Ours-It's quite far. Portsmouth-not far from Southampton." *Southampton.* Maybe I would get to meet Amber somehow and ask about David and Ella. I started getting ideas of how I could meet Amber.

"There's a really nice beach as well that we'd like to take you to for a picnic." Said the lady, practically my soon-to-be mum. "My name is Jasmine, and my husband's here's name is Ayad. "Said the lady, well, Jasmine. Her name suited her Perfectly. Jasmine had pretty hazel eyes. I looked around the car. There were three girls in the middle, and I and he girl next to me were behind them. They seemed really interested in me, staring thoughtfully at me, so I had to keep that smile plastered on my face. After all, I didn't want to make a bad impression in my first five minutes. Ayad started driving the car and we were off. Everyone back at the Burton House was still in the window, waving me goodbye. As far as I was concerned there were no boys there.

That meant no annoying boys like James and Brandon. "Hi, "said the girl shyly next to me. She was definitely my age. We did the usual 'what's your name? my name is this. what's yours?' I'd done that routine too many times in my life. I was an expert at this sort of stuff. Her name was Camila. "It's a shame - my brothers didn't come. They're so funny."

"*Brothers*?" I said, shocked. Well, all I could do was pray they weren't annoying little brothers.

"Yeah-Aziz and Ali," she said.

"Why didn't they come?"

I asked. "Aziz- he's twenty-two and he went to work-he works at a special police force. And Ali-he's eighteen. He works at a stadium."

"A stadium," I gasped.

"Like, a football stadium." She nodded.

"That's so cool!" I exclaimed.

"Mum told me I would be going to school with you. I'm going to be in your year. We're going to year eight. Which school did you go to? What did you do on your last day of year six?"

I smiled. She was a curious one.

"Well, it's a long story. What if, when I move in with you next week, I'll tell you at bedtime." She squealed excitedly. "That would be great. I can't wait."

"What are you?" Asked the sixteen-year-old girl, facing me. She'd been playing games on her phone a few minutes ago. I was taken aback by this question. Was she trying to be funny? "I'm a human."

"No, silly," She laughed. "Are you Christian or are you a Jew or are you a..."

"Muslim, "I said. "Didn't they tell you?" I asked. "Maybe they told mum." She said.

"She's got an Arabic name." Said Ayad.

"Arabic?" I asked.

"Forget it.," Camila Said. "We don't want to confuse you already." She took out a few pieces of paper from her purple hoodies pocket. "These are the pictures I took when I went to Algeria. *Algeria.* "

"I'm Algerian," I said.

"Really? That's such a coincidence. We're Algerian too. "Said Camila. We carried on talking, me telling her about the orphanage and me going to school only to year four. I tried hinting there was something wrong there and she caught on very well. "I really want to know, but I guess I'll have to wait till next week. You know, two days after you move in with us, we'll be going to school with us."

"The holidays are already ending. Well, it's been a long one- loads of crazy things have happened to me this holiday."

"Tell me!"

"The wait will be worth it, I'm telling you." If you are a Muslim, why don't you wear a scarf?" Said a little girl, on one side of the girl with the phone. She looked five or six. "Oh...err..." I didn't know what to say.

"Don't be so rude. "Said the girl on the other side. She was probably seven or eight.

"I'm not being rude. I was just asking. "The little girl said.

"You were being rude."

"No, I wasn't."

"Yes, you were."

"Alright, girls, enough with that." Said Jasmine. I could feel myself turning red. Camila introduced me to all her sisters. The sixteen-year-old was Sumayyah, the five-year olds name was Amirah and the other girl- the who was eight was called Abida. The journey was long over two hours. I fell asleep during the last part of the journey.

"Wake up. We're here." said Camila. I opened my eyes. There was a black gate with gold diamond shapes on top of each bar. "Your house has a gate. That's so cool."

I exclaimed. The gate opened automatically and we drove to the parking area next to the house. The house itself was hugely looking. It was three floors high.

"We'll give you a tour of the house - just so you kind of know where you're going when you come next week. "Said Ayad. It was him, Jasmine and the little one-Amirah. She held my hand.

"Can I show her my room?" She asked, looking at Jasmine.

"Yeah, in a bit," Jasmine replied. Amirah held my hand tighter and looked up excitedly at me. We went inside, and there was a short corridor. Straight ahead were the stairs, and on the right, there were three doors. They took me to the room at the very end of the corridor. "This is the living room." Said Jasmine. She opened the door and we stepped in. I gave a little gasp. It was huge. Bigger than Ella's living room and Maddie's living room squashed into one. It was long as it was wide and had the really fluffy modern grey carpet. There was a circle rug in the middle-a baby blue rug, and there were grey sofas. There was a glass table in the middle.

There was a large TV on the wall and underneath it was two large house plants-one on each side. "Out of all t he living rooms I've seen, this is by far the best," I said. Ayad smiled proudly. "All my Idea. Jasmine wanted us to have plain wooden floors and Brown leather chairs. Not *my* idea of decorating a living room." Jasmine shook her head slowly and I giggled. There were double-glazed windows which led to the garden. We went outside.

"Once, mummy wanted to do a barbecue outside, but then she burnt all the sausages and everything else." Giggled Amirah. She was still holding my hands, which was cold against my warm fingers. I was boiling in my black culottes and white top, with my long, black cardigan. Amirah's hands were nice and cold. For such a hot day as well. The first thing that met my eyes when I saw the garden was the massive swimming pool on the floor. There were a few benches around it, with swings further down the garden. On the other side of the garden was a wooden balcony, with deck chairs on it.

"Once, my husband was fixing the deck chairs on the balcony and before we realised he'd plunged into the pool. "Said Jasmine, laughing." I grinned. I realised they were trying to embarrass each other as retaliation.

"Now can I show Aleena my room?" Amirah Asked. "Yes. I'll get my special doughnuts while we wait." Said Jasmine.

"Mummy's a doughnut lady. She has a shop called 'Dainty Doughnuts'. The doughnuts are so yummy!"

"I'm sure they are!" I said. She was so adorable- her hand curled around my two fingers, swinging my arm as we walked across the landing. I was glad she was going to be *my* sister soon. She opened a door.

"This is my room!" She said, clearly thinking the world of it. It looked just as I imagined. A typical five-year-old bedroom. Everything was *pink*. Her walls were pink, her carpet was pink with a pink rug, her bed and bed covers were pink, and her teddy bear was pink. She even had a pink bedside cabinet and light. When she turned the light on, light purple and blue stars covered the ceiling.

"This is so cute!" I said. And I meant it-though it wasn't really *my* dream room.

"Yeah!" Amirah replied, hopping up and down.

"It took mummy and dad the whole weekend to do my bedroom."

"Woah, that's a long time. Where would my room be?" I asked. "Oh, you can't see your room yet," She smiled. "It's a surprise. Mummy and dad are deco..."

"She clasped her hand over her mouth and looked at me guiltily.

"Oh, I wasn't meant to say anything. Please don't say that I told you.

I laughed. "Alright."

"Let's go back then. "She said.

"Ok." She ran off. I followed behind her.

"Did you like Amirah's room? "Asked Ayad.
"Yeah," I said. "It's really pretty."
"Oh, it took us our whole weekend." Said Jasmine as we walked back out. As we neared the car, I could hear Camila, Sumayyah and Abida fighting. An argument. Amirah giggled and squeezed my hand as Ayad and Jasmine looked at each other. As soon as we reached the car, I saw Sumayyah give Abiah a quick slap. Ayad opened

the door for me. I went in, smiling at Camila. She was trying to stifle her laughter- I could see why. Sumayyah could be seen in the driver's mirror, turning red. "So, we're going to the beach!" Ayad exclaimed.

"Yay!"

"I love the beach!"

"This is the best day ever!"

"I can't wait!" Amirah and Abida were making a lot of racket, but it was funny. I wished they were my real family. One thing that occupied my mind the whole time was how I wished for these people to be my real family. It could have been the slightest bit possible, though. We were both Algerian, and my surname *was* Ayad. I had green eyes like Ayad too. But I knew it couldn't be possible. If they were really my family, Ayad and Jasmine definitely wouldn't have put me in an orphanage. What would be the reason?

"Well, did you like Amirah's room?" Camila asked. I looked at Amirah, who was chatting happily with Sumayyah. "It's really nice-really...pink."

"Yeah, not my best pick, but nice enough for her age. Hey, do you mind having your own room?" Camila asked.

"No, why?" I asked.

"Nothing. Just asking."

Ok. So, I'm gonna be having my own room. Things couldn't get *any* better. I've always wanted to have my own room. I could have all the things I wanted. It would be my first time *not* sharing a room.

"We're here!" Cried Jasmine.

Chapter 25

I looked around. It was rocky. Loads of pebbles.

"We were *planning* to go to a sandy beach, but *apparently,* it got fully covered in water... from the sea, obviously." Said Ayad.

We got out. The first thing that hit me was Ella. I couldn't help it.

All I could think of was when she took me to the beach. As soon as we reached it, the salty smell of the sea hit me. That's what happened this time. I scrunched up my nose. "I made something special for the picnic-specially for you. Hope you enjoy it! Sumayyah was right next to me, but her eyes were glued to the phone as she spoke. I couldn't help peeking at her phone.

"What game is that? "I asked before zipping my mouth shut. "I'm sorry...I didn't mean to look at your phone. I... I just..." I said.

"Oh, it's fine. You can have a turn whilst we wait for mum and dad."

"Oh, thanks...what's it called?" I asked.

"Dodger." She replied. *Dodger?*

"How do you play*?" I* asked.

"You swipe to the right to go right to switch lanes, collect gold and dodge the chickens- you can swipe to the left to do the same. You swipe down to roll underneath broken bridges, double tap to jump really high. You have to try to get to the temple first-you see all those blobs-they're other players."

Camila came up to us. "Hey, you never let me play on your phone!"

"Because you don't even know how to play. You're dead in two seconds anyways." replied Sumayyah.

"Sumayyah, if you don't mind, can I see who wins between you and Camila?"

"Of course, though, this will be too funny." Replied Sumayyah.

"I'll start." Said Camila. She took the phone off me and started to play. But it was true. Her Blob kept bumping into other Blobs. She always forgot to switch lanes and roll under bridges. "See, told you. You've seen me play- you don't need to see again," said Sumayyah.

"What are your parents doing?" I asked. They were fussing with Abida, but I couldn't quite see what they were doing. "Oh, they're putting Abida in her wheelchair," Camila replied.

"Her wheelchair?"

"Yeah. Its' because she's disabled. She can't walk." She said.

"OH! That's so sad...umm..." I didn't know what else to say.

"They're coming now." Said Camila. She looked so sad.

"Let's go!" Said Ayad. He held the picnic in his left hand and held Amirah on his right shoulder. Jasmine was pushing the wheelchair. Sumayyah ran up next to her and began chatting with her.

I walked with Camila, who told me all about the funny pranks her year pulled on their year six teacher in the last week of year six. I was bursting to tell her about pranks I used to play on my friends in the orphanage. But I promised I'd save it for next week.

We got a spot. Ayad lowered Amirah to the ground and spread the picnic mat. Summary helped him unpack the food from the basket whilst Jasmine settled Abida. Amirah ran up to me.

"Come and sit!" I let her pull me to the mat. I sat next to her. Camila sat next to me.

"That's Mahjouba - Algerian crepes. It tastes so nice!"

"It looks really nice. What type of Algerian food do you like most? What do you like eating for breakfast?" I asked Amirah and Camila.

"Shakshouka!" They replied in unison.

"What's Shakshouka?"

"Are you a fan of eggs?" Asked Camila.

"Yeah-I *love* it."

"Well, it's like-it's basically poached eggs in a tomato sauce with other spices and herbs. It's so nice- when you come next week, if you come in the morning, I'll tell mum to make it for you as your first breakfast. And if you come at night, I'll ask mum if she can cook it in the morning. What do you say?"

"Oh, I'd love that!"

"We have some other dishes," Said Abida, wheeling her wheelchair towards us,

"I asked mum to make it. Look, there's Bourek *and* my favourite dessert- Qalb el Louz." They all sounded so cool, but I didn't know what they were. Bourek was a pie-like pastry with different fillings. These ones were filled with meat, potatoes and cheese. Qalb el Louz was made of semolina, honey, orange blossoms and almonds. It looked the slightest bit like cake, but sweeter and not spongy like cake, either.

"This is the special thing I made- my speciality." Said Sumayyah, sitting opposite me.

"It looks good. What is it?" I asked.

"Peri- peri chicken wings."

"Sumayyah makes the bestest bestest chicken wings ever!" Said Amirah.

"Yes, she does. And she does a good job of messing the whole kitchen too." Said Jasmine.

"Mum!" Said Sumayyah, looking embarrassed.

"Don't worry; you'll grow up to be the best chicken wing cooker ever." Said Ayad.

Chapter 26

Every Algerian dish I tried was delicious. I was keen on trying Chakhchoukha - It had pieces of thin flat bread, with a stew with tomatoes, chickpeas, diced lamb pieces and some other spice. Jasmine promised to make it on the night I came.

After the picnic, it had already turned six o'clock. We all sat in silence, watching the children run around, people surfing in the sea and hundreds of seagulls flying across our heads, stealing people's bread.

The sea was two different colours-a murky brown water in front of blue water. They started asking me questions about myself and I pulled out a picture of myself when I was a baby. Jasmine and Ayad looked at each other and smiled. I felt ready to be a part of this family. Quite a long few hours ago I was zero percent happy about going to this new family of mine, but now I actually liked them.

When it reached seven o'clock, we started packing up and heading to the van. I offered to push Abida's wheelchair and she delightedly agreed. While Ayad lifted her into the van, I watched Jasmine fold up her wheelchair. It was a nice-ish colour- pastel pink -though she didn't really like the colour. Her favourite colour was purple.

Jasmine held my hand and brought me closer to her. I could smell the Jasmine scent on her like I did when I first met her. "You are one remarkable girl. I'll be proud to have you as a daughter soon."

"Thank you," I said. I was kind of hoping that she would say,' *I think this is the right time to tell you this. You're my daughter. My biological daughter."* I got into the car and sat beside Camila. Her eyes were drooping.

"I better say bye to you now 'because I think I'm gonna fall asleep. I probably won't be able to say it to you then." I smiled.

"I'll be looking forward to seeing you again next week-won't have to say goodbye to me then."

"Yeah."

The drive back seemed so quick. It barely felt like half an hour, though the actual journey took over two hours. We stopped outside the house. Jasmine said it was almost ten o'clock. "By the way, what's your favourite colour-just out of interest."

"Well, I have quite a few."

"Name them all."

"Well, I'm more into light blue, light green- pastel and mint and also light purple. But then I'm not *too* keen on purple. I got out of the van, putting my hand in my pocket, making sure my picture was there. Everyone except Jasmine, Sumayyah and obviously Ayad were sleeping. I waved them goodbye. Ayad walked me up to the doorstep. Justin opened the door. I said bye to Ayad and entered inside. Justin shut the door and moved out of the way, revealing everybody's eager faces, dying to know what happened.

"How was it?" Asked Marie.

"Great! It was really nice-I even got to taste a few Algerian foods."

"Wow! Did you like the food?" Asked Rose.

"Yeah, Jasmine is going to make me a special dish for me the day I go to live there."

"Well! In just four days, you'll be going-unless you want to make it sound longer and say next week." Said Ava.

To be honest, I was really excited to move in with them, so I didn't want to think of it as next week. To me, four days sounded quicker. But not wanting to offend anyone, I didn't say anything. Brandon and James went off to bed. "Well, I think you should all go back to your rooms and go to sleep. Aleena must be very tired now." Said Justin. So, we all made our way upstairs.

"Are you excited to go?" Whispered Maddy after we were all tucked in bed.

"Yeah! I'm so excited. I'm gonna have my own room and..." I heard a sad sigh come from her.

"...but I'm gonna miss you lot a lot. Especially you." I don't know what her reaction was, but it was as if I could feel her smile vibrating around me.

" G'night." She whispered.

"G'night," I whispered back.

Chapter 27

Two days whizzed past, and the third day came. The second to last day before I went to live in Portsmouth. We went on a canoeing trip, which was fun. "The last time we went canoeing, we all fell in the water!" Laughed Harmony.

"I'm still not sure about this water," Said Rose, looking scared.

"Scaredy cat. There are no crocodiles in this lake." Said Brandon.

"Or maybe there are!" James said, winking at Brandon. Then, he jumped, making the whole canoe tilt.

"Stop! If we fall inside...who knows which hungry crocodile will see us as a tasty lunch?" Shouted Rose, clinging onto Ava.

"B... but I swear I just saw one...teeth up...near our canoe!" Said James, making himself stutter. I sat there, enjoying the scene. Rose squealed and jumped onto Ava's lap. "Get off!"

"I'm so scared!"

"Get *off*!"

"O*kay.*"

"Don't worry, James is just pulling your leg." Said Justin.

"No, he's not." Replied Rose.

Justin looked confused, then said, "No, not physically, as in, he's like...you know...ugh, just forget it."

"What your dad is trying to say," Said Marie, "Is that James is just teasing you."

"Yeah, that," Justin said.

"Oh." Replied Rose. After the trip, we went back home. Marie made her special cheesy potato pastry with omelette and beans for dinner. For me, it tasted better than it sounded. My last dinner with them. After dinner, I went upstairs to pack my backpack. I never really had anything important. Just my workhouse clothes, my baby picture (which I still found a bit weird having that on me) and a few pounds left. We had to do all the goodbyes. My last goodbyes. "Bye."

"We'll miss you."

"Take care."

"Have fun."

"Stay in touch!"

"Don't miss me too much!" I said before going to bed. That night I couldn't sleep. I was excited to go. Very excited. I had to go to bed early -at eight o clock at night. Way too early for me. But I was heading for my new home at six a.m in the morning.

Then I could arrive at eight or nine in the morning. I slipped off to sleep eventually. It felt like I'd slept for only a minute. Marie came in to wake me up. I had to get ready and leave. My last sleep here.

"Bye darling. It was nice having you here." Said Marie. Her voice a soft whisper.

"Thank you," I replied.

"Wait!" A loud whisper came from the stairs. It was Maddy. She ran up to me and hugged me. I hugged her back. "Bye, I'll miss you. Safe travel."

"Thank you," I replied.

"And thank you. For everything, you've done. Especially...yeah."

I nodded, catching on to what she meant.

"Okay, Maddy. Time or you to go." Said Marie as she led me outside to the van. It was quite chilly. I wrapped my coat tighter around me. Marie and Ayad spoke a bit and exchanged files. Marie handed him some sheets of paper. He signalled for me to get in the van. Marie gave a quick wave and rushed indoors. "Well, let's take you home. To your *real* home," Said Ayad as he started the car.

The car journey was a long journey, but I slept the whole way through. It was finally happening. I never for once thought in my life that this would happen. When we finally reached the automatic gate, it opened. Ayad parked his van and took out my bags. I waited for him to open the door to the house. The door to a new life. I went inside to see Jasmine waiting at the door.

The first thing my eyes fell upon was the bunting. *'Welcome to your new family.'* It said

"Come in, come in." said Jasmine. I followed her into another room. In the corridor, there was a door next to the living room door. I went through it and there was a kitchen and dining room attached to each other. Everyone was at the table- even the brothers. *My* brother's. And that's what made me even more nervous. And worst of all, they were grinning from ear to ear. I was quite sure they could hear my heart beating fast. "Sit next to me! "Said Abida.

"No! Sit next to me!" Shouted Amirah. I fought back the urge to laugh. The seat that Abida and Amirah were pointing at was in between the two of them.

Either way, I would be sitting side by side with both of them. One of the boys-one of my brothers laughed out loud. I guessed it was Aziz-the older one-he looked older than the other one. "She's still gonna sit next to you both." He said. Ali, I was guessing, began laughing loudly, and then everyone started laughing. He had a very contagious laugh. There's no way he's gonna laugh without you laughing as well.

"Umm...where do I put my bag?" I asked Jasmine.

"Is that all you got?"

"No, I've got another bag."

"Oh, then. We'll put it in the living room for now." Ayad took my things into the living room whereas I went and sat in between Amirah and Abida. Jasmine went to the kitchen and brought a pot whilst Sumayyah handed out plates. Jasmine opened the pot. A load of steam went flying out. Once the steam had gone, I looked at what was in the pot. Shakshouka! I almost forgot. I was dying to taste it and so far, it smelt wonderful.

She served me first. "Enjoy!" I was dying to try it, but I decided to wait for everyone to get served first. After everyone got their serving, Jasmine handed out Challah- a 'criss-cross bread', as Amirah called it. Really, it was plaited bread, and it was really nice. "So, how do you like it?" Asked Camila. I tried to sound confident, but it came out more like a croaky whisper.

"Yeah."

"Better than pancakes, then?" She asked. I told her on the beach trip that pancakes were my favourite breakfast. "Definitely! One hundred percent."

This time it come out confident, but my voice went strangely deep. I wanted the floor to swallow me there and then. It was so embarrassing and I was sure I saw Ali smirking.

"No need to be embarrassed, little one." Ali said. I forgot all my embarrassment and nervousness. "I'm not nervous and I'm *not* little," I said. Ali looked taken aback. Then I remembered how I called Brandon 'little one'. I wouldn't dare call Amirah that. She was cute, but she seemed to have a fiery personality if you triggered her. I wouldn't call Abida that either. I felt as if I couldn't do anything to upset her at all.

She seemed so fragile and vulnerable in her chair next to me. "I *like* her," Said Aziz, grinning. "She's a feisty one!"

"Thank you," I replied, grinning back. After breakfast, Jasmine and Ayad told us all to go upstairs. Then they helped me take my bags to *my new* bedroom.

Everyone, including my brothers, gathered around to see my reaction as soon as I opened the door. As soon as I did, my jaw dropped open. This was not what I expected at all. In fact, it was even better than I expected. My jaw was hanging. "Do you like it?" Asked Jasmine and Ayad in unison. I looked them in the eye.

"I love it! Thank you so much!" Everyone began cheering. We went into the room. I saw what a massive room it was. Everybody pointed out what they did- including Amirah, who painted a little gold star on the ceiling. The whole room was perfect. There was not a single fault I could pull out -not that I wanted to pull out any.

The whole room was pastel blue, with sage green curtains. There was a double bed, with a little white bedside cabinet next to it. At the foot of my bed was a silver velvet upholstered bench. The carpet was a pale green, with a Darker green rug.

Then there was the wooden wardrobe. Then the little wooden stand with a picture on it. I couldn't stop smiling the whole way. This was *my* bedroom. The light purple lamp just blended in perfectly too. Ayad and Jasmine left, but everyone else stayed. They told me to tell them all my stories whilst I unpacked. I groaned. I had a lot of unpacking to do. Marie dumped the bag with all my clothes in, in the van. As I unpacked, I told the story right from the beginning, all the way to the end. Like in Maddie's house, everyone gave the same reactions.

"You are one crazy girl," Said Ali. "You really escaped!"

"How do you have the guts to do that...I couldn't. If I were your friend, Maddy, I would have ditched you!" Said Sumayyah.

"No surprise," Said Aziz to Sumayyah. "No wonder you have no friends."

"Be quiet, you don't know!" Retorted Sumayyah.

Amirah looked frightened. "Is it real? Is it all true? Every single bit?"

"Yes," I replied earnestly.

"What's gonna happen to Ella?" Asked Abida. She was sitting on my bed.

"Poor her!" Added Camila.

"I don't know," I said. "I wish there was a way to help them. My heart never stops thundering when I think of it."

"So, this whole situation is real, you say?" Aziz said.

"Yep."

"I could do something about it. I could get David out of prison if that's what you say."

"You can?" I piped out.

"Though it could take some time. I work in a special police force department. But still, there could be a low chance of finding him."

"That sounds like he can't be helped to me." I said.

"No, no, it's just a possibility. And I'll try to get you involved as less as I can."

"Okay." All the packing was done. Everyone went outside, whilst Camila offered to do a tour of the house.

The top two floors were spacious- four bedrooms and one bathroom on each Floor. Eight bedrooms altogether. I'd mastered the bottom floor, though. She pointed out her room, which was similar to mine but with different colour combinations. Blush pink and dark blue. Then Sumayyah room, though we didn't go in. I already saw Amirah's room.

Then on the top floor were Abida's room, Aziz's room and Ali's room and her parent's room. "Now, I'll show you our school uniform." It looked alright. Dark blue trousers, dark blue blazer with a white lining, Dark blue ties and black shoes.

Brriinngg.

"That must be our uncle!" Cried Camila.

"Your who?"

"Our first guest to come and see you. Mum and Dad invited all our relatives."

"Oh, Ummm..."

“Come, let's go!”

Chapter 28

"Hello there!" Said the uncle. "I'm uncle Kadir."

"Hi."

"How are you?"

"Good." He left and went to Ayad and Jasmine. I didn't want to meet anyone else. I didn't know why I was so nervous, but I was. Amirah ran up to me with a tennis racket.

"Can you play tennis with me? No one wants to play with me."

"Sure." I could kind of see why no one wanted to play with her. She kept whacking the ball high into the sky, or she'd throw the ball without batting it. But I didn't mind. It was cute and funny. Sumayyah was on her laptop outside, typing out something. Aziz was pushing Abida around in her wheelchair. Ali was doing keep uppish with his football, clearly flexing.

Camila was watching us play. We played the same game for hours, whilst many visitors came. We had the same conversation over and over again. Uncle Kadir-I figured out he was Jasmine's only brother and Ayad's best friend.

There were too many aunties, though- Aunty Sophie, Aunty Zarah, Aunty Aakifa, Aunty Nadia and Aunty Sadia, who were twins and lots more. Ayad had loads of brothers too. Later, all the Aunties, uncles and *my* family sat on the floor in a big circle and began to eat. Jasmine made roast potatoes, Chakhchoukha and a chicken and mushroom risotto.

It was like I'd be tasting new food every day. After dinner, everyone but Uncle Kadir left.

He beckoned me outside. "This is for you. This locket. It holds something very important. You are a smart girl, I know. Don't open it. And I mean it. Don't open it till you know the time is right. And don't tell anyone I gave this to you. The time will come very soon."

"Ok. Thank you, Uncle."

"You're welcome." He placed the locket in my hand before closing it. I smiled. He kissed my forehead and then left. I waited for him to get into his car and waved goodbye before going inside. "What did your uncle tell you?" Jasmine Asked.

"Oh...he just told me he knows I'm a smart girl and I should make my parents proud. And I will." I said. I mean, *some* of it was true. She smiled.

"You're just the perfect child, aren't you?" She said, squeezing my cheeks. "Beautiful, smart, funny and confident." I could feel my cheeks burning, and I was fighting the urge to break free from her, especially when Aziz snorted and nudged Ali, who was grinning madly. I could feel my face burning. "It's late now. I think you lot should go to bed now." Said Ayad, helping me out.

Everybody got up except Aziz and Ali. "We'll be up in a moment." Said Aziz. They looked so much like Ayad- just they didn't have his green eyes. I followed everyone and offered to help Abida to her room. She seemed only too happy. I waved her goodnight and went to Amirah's room, which was between mine and Sumayyah's room. Camila's room was on my other side. Amirah grinned. "Can you tell me a story?" She asked.

"Ok, what type of story."

"About a monster who eats humans. Then one day the knight comes and saves the humans and defeats the monster." I shut the room door and walked inside. I sat at the foot of her bed, shocked. That was the least thing i was expecting her to say.

"Won't you get nightmares?" I asked.

"No. Well, yes, maybe. What about princesses and knights and dragons."

"Ok." So, I unravelled a story about her being a princess, locked up in castle by a dragon, but the knight came and saved her. "I like that story," She said sleepily.

"Can you tell it again tomorrow and the day after and the day after forever?"

"Of course," I said, heading towards the door. "Goodnight."

"G, night." She replied. I turned her light off, leaving her pink lamp light.

"You've already made her sleep?" Asked Jasmine, stunned as I headed towards my room. I stopped. "Yeah. I told her a story."

"Well, I think you should give her stories more often. It takes us years to get her to sleep."

I smiled.

"Goodnight." Whispered Jasmine.

"Goodnight," I replied. As soon as I entered my room, the cosy feeling returned to me. The fluffy carpet I was standing on right now was something. A few months ago,

If someone told me I was gonna be living in this luxury, I wouldn't have believed them for a second. But now, here I was.

Chapter 29

The first day of year eight came. I held my locket. Not for luck, but out of excitement. It was a pretty little thing-it was a circle shape which could open, attached to a necklace. I put it back in my drawer.

When would the right time come? Someone knocked. "Come in?" It was Camila.

"Well, you make me *envious*. Every single outfit you wear suits you well. Even *uniform.*" I laughed.

"I'll take that as a compliment."

"You're welcome." She replied.

"Hey! You do your scarf so nicely. Teach me!"

"Are you just trying to compliment me because I..."

"No, no, promise. I tried yesterday night and I looked like an embarrassment."

"Ok." She wrapped it around my hair until it was tight and fitted well.

"Much better." I said.

"Thanks." My French braids weren't a very popular thing in this house. Everyone could do it-even Amirah. But Ella's cornrows were. They were similar- but not the same.

"Let's go down for breakfast!" Said Camila. We went down. Amirah and Abida were already there. They both had grey pinafores and red cardigans. "Well! Your all jumping up the years!" Said Ayad. "Yes! I'm going to be in year one! And soon, I'll be in big school!"

"Me too!" Said Abida. Jasmine laughed.

"Yes, you will. And you'll be very tall too."

"Taller than daddy?" Asked Amirah.

"Much, much taller than him." Amirah and Abida giggled. I and Camila helped ourselves to some coco pops. Jasmine and Ayad told me to call them mum and dad, which was very exciting, but it was really hard to, especially since I wasn't used to it. Ayad took us to school whilst Jasmine took Abida and Amirah to their school.

We stopped at the front gate.

"What type of school is this?" I asked.

"A girl's school. This one was rated *outstanding*."

"Oh...Okay."

"Ok, bye. I'm gonna go now." Said Ayad, as the gates opened.

"Hey, Camila!" Said a girl. She had red hair, blue eyes and lots of freckles.

"HI!" Camila replied. I followed her to where we were meant to be.

"Who's this?" The girl asked, smiling at me.

"This is Aleena-new girl of year eight."

"Oh, hi Aleena. My name is Brittany."

"Nice to meet you," I replied.

"Aren't you meant to be going through the office?' Cause your new." I stopped.

"Really?"

"Oh no! Dad forgot to take you to the office." Said Camila.

"It's fine! We'll take you." Said Brittany. We turned back and made our way to the office. The lady at the office took a long time to find my name, but eventually, she did and lead us to our class. I prayed to be in the same class as Camila. "You're in this class," Said the office lady as she pointed at a grey door.

"Camila, Brittany, back to your own class." This was the moment to be nervous. I didn't have Camila with me. What would I do?

She opened the door. And told me to follow her inside. She murmured to the teacher at the desk. "This is the new girl." She left. The teacher walked up to me. She had short blonde hair and brown eyes, with rectangle glasses. She has dressed up really...oddly. Rainbow top with green and black chequered trousers. Didn't match, but that wasn't my problem. She looked friendly enough, though, so I wasn't put off together. "Everybody, this is our new girl, Aleena."

"Hello, Aleena." They all said.

"I want you all to be nice to her." She said. Like they had an option. By the end of the day, they would all be my friend. And I knew it.

"Where should you sit?" She whispered, scanning the room.

"Miss, she can sit next to me!" Said a girl. She had large grey eyes and curly blonde hair. She stood up as she spoke.

"Okay then, Aleena. You can go and sit there." I went to sit next to her. She smiled warmly and I smiled back.

"My name is Scarlet. Nice to meet you." She whispered.

"Nice to meet you too." The day wasn't too bad. We didn't really do any learning- just handing out new books and doing tests. I knew I would fail the test. I hadn't been to school since year *four*. Break time finally came. I was dying to go and see Camila. But I didn't think I'd be able to.

Everyone kept turning back, sending me notes to see me at break time, catching my eye to smile at me. All except one. I went outside with Scarlet, scanning the field desperately. It was way different to primary school, where the field was concrete and there were lots of play equipment.

Camila ran up to me. "There you are! I was looking for you everywhere. I could feel your nervousness, almost as if I was nervous too!"

"Don't worry, I had Scarlet here with me the whole time."

"I'll leave you two to talk." Said Scarlet.

"No, wait. It'll be a minute." I said.

"Who *is* Brittany?" I asked.

"My best friend." Replied Camila.

"Oh...Okay. Just wanted to know. Bye." I went to Scarlet.

"Who *is* Camila to you?"

"My sister," I said, without hesitation.

"Oh, so you're twins."

"No-it's complicated," I replied.

"Hey, Aleena." Said a girl, she came with a group of girls- practically my whole class.

"Hi," I said. I wasn't shy, or nervous.

They were my age. Why should I be?

"Nice to meet you. My name is Alexia."

"Nice to meet you, Alexia." She began pointing out everyone's names. I pointed out everyone's name, just to clarify. "Woah, you've got a brain in a million." Said a girl called Sally.

"I know right? Were like -thirty girls and you know who we all are." We went back inside.

The one girl who didn't like me sat at the front and stuck out her tongue when I walked past. "Childish," I whispered to Scarlet. She grinned in response.

"Who is she?" I asked.

"Olive," whispered Scarlet. The hour dragged by until finally, it was lunch break. Lunch was what I expected. three options - vegetarian, not vegetarian, or jacket potatoes. Roast potatoes with ham, gravy and new peas or roast potatoes with Quorn sausages, gravy and new peas. I had the second option. Ayad and Jasmine told me about how Muslims don't eat pigs.

Everyone, including Olive, sat with me in the dining room, though she kept her distance. There was jelly and Ice cream, but I didn't like the look of the green jelly. Olive seemed to love hers.

"Olive, do you want my jelly and ice cream?" Everyone gasped. Her face lit up.

"She hates your guts to bits for some reason. She's gonna take advantage of you now." Whispered Scarlet. "No, she won't. And if she tries, I'll put her back in her place - where she belongs." I whispered back.

"Oh, yes please." Said, Olive. She was like a whole other person when she said *please*.

"She'll feel guilty now for sticking her tongue out at me, just wait," I said, getting up.

Camila had just gone out with a group of her classmates. I went to her. "How is it so far?" She asked.

"Great." Her friends smiled at me. We had to do the usual routine of introducing ourselves and the 'nice to meet you part as well.

"How do you like this school?" Said Emily. She was a really tall girl with short copper hair and glasses.

"I like it a lot." My classmates came up to me. For some reason, I tried to see if Olive was there too. But she wasn't. She walked off to the other side of the field nose in the air. Maybe Scarlet was right. "What do you want to play, Aleena?" Asked Alexia.

"I don't mind. But I do like Bulldog?" They all looked quizzical.

"Gladiator?"

"Still don't know what you're talking about." Said Alexia.

"Everyone stands on one end and you have to run to the other end without getting caught by whoever is in the middle. If you do get caught, you stay in the middle and catch other people. Then we'll see the last person to run."

"Okay. You stay in the middle." Said Scarlet.

"Okay." Halfway through Camila's class joined in, making in the whole of year eight playing. A few years seven's joined too, while year nines and tens watched. I *felt* like a proud *sister* when Camila won the last person running. The rest of school dragged, but it finally ended.

"Sumayyah will walk with us home." Said Camila.

"Okay." Brittany lived a street away, while Scarlet lived opposite us. Brittany gave me her Mento which she snuck into school and ate with Camila through class time. I realised quite a lot of people from our school lived near us.

"How was it?" Asked Jasmine when we came back.

"It was lovely," I said.

"Oh lord! What happened to your uniform?" Asked Sumayyah, picking up Amirah.

"I spilt baked beans on it."

Sumayyah laughed. "Let's get you changed then." We had to pray, which was something I was still getting used to. It was interesting though. "We go to another school after school." Said Camila.

"What school?"

"Madrasah." Said Sumayyah. "Tell her, Camila."

"We learn-you know, like school but Muslim wise-Islamic wise."

"Look." Ayad came upstairs. "Dad, you didn't take Aleena to the office." said Camila.

"Oh...what did the office say?"

"Me and Brittany took her there, but the office didn't seem to notice."

"Oh, sorry about that." Said Ayad. I smiled. We went downstairs and Jasmine was there. She made couscous for us. I was surprised I could eat since I had lunch not that long ago. Aziz came in and sat with us. "Aleena, I have news." Said Aziz.

"What news?" Asked Ali.

"Hey!" I said.

"I have bad news and bad news and good news." Said Aziz. He looked at me very seriously.

"I want the bad news," I said.

"Typical." Said Ali.

"Well," Said Aziz, "The first bad news is that they cannot find this David you're talking about. And the other bad news is that I can't tell you the good news."

"Oh... o*kay*...," "I said, confused.

"Don't worry," said Ali. "Good things come to those who wait."

"I guess so." I said. And he was right.

Chapter 30

When I came back from madrassah, there was a surprise waiting. "David? Amber? Ella." I didn't know how to react. Thank god, David was out of prison, but how would they feel about me-it was all my fault, after all.

"Let's talk." Said Amber. I led them to the living room. Everyone left the living room, leaving me, David, Ella and Amber. It was so awkward.

"Let's just start by saying," Said David, breaking the silence, "That I didn't go to prison."

"What? Come again? I don't understand...how?"

"I'll explain, as simply as I can." Said David. Ella came and sat next to me.

"Oh, I've missed you." She said. She hugged me hard.

"What happened? This is so confusing." I said.

"Well, the guy who drove you in the taxi, he was actually meant to take you to your friend Maddie's house. That was not an orphanage he was taking you to. It was to cover up the plan. But you made it harder for them by running away.

We never knew about all this. We only found out all this the day before I was "arrested". They tracked you down until they found out where you were. They found out on that day and came straight to us, telling us the plan."

"So, they told you about it the day before you were 'arrested'?" I asked.

"Yes. That nurse at the hospital with Maddy was part of the plan. Part of the Mayors' plan."

"*The Mayor?*"

"Yeah. He only helped the Mossy lady 'cause he and his son and this community group looking for families for all you lot. Some were happily reunited. Some were not.

He didn't want it to look like he was helping you, so he made us act. That's why we were telling you to run."

"Oh...I was wondering why you did that." I said.

"Yeah. Well, little miss Mossy will be taken to court in a few weeks, once they get everyone out of that workhouse. She's still oblivious of what's going on." Said Amber, grinning.

"I would love to give her a piece of my mind," I said.

"Well, we thought we'd just tell you this," David said, getting up.

"Right." I said, getting up.

"How was the internship thing by the way?"

"Oh, it was good." Said David.

"And we both got the job!" Said Amber excitedly.

"That's great," I said.

"Maybe next time we'll come again and you can tell us what you got up to after you left us."

"Okay. Bye." I shut the door. Everybody came up to me.

"That was the good news I couldn't tell you." Said Aziz.

I smiled. "It was very good news."

Chapter 31

The second day of year eight went smoothly, with a couple of surprises. Olive left a note on my desk apologising and stuck a packet of sweets under my desk.

I took it gratefully and shared it with her, Brittany, Camila, Scarlet and Sumayyah on the way back home. Madrassah went pretty well too. I was in a lower year, but my teacher said I would go to my normal year soon because I had '*a sharp brain*'. Afterwards, was the talk.

"We often do this, when we want to share our secrets. It's like letting you into our family secrets." Said Jasmine. We all sat in a circle on the floor in the living room.

"This one is not something everyone knows about. Sumayyah has a slight memory of it. Aziz and Ali have full knowledge of it, I'm sure." She said.

"You see, I once had twins. Ayad brought a photo of a family-there was Ayad, Jasmine, Aziz and Ali, Sumayyah, Uncle Kadir and Aunty Sofia and two babies-the twins."

"Camila was one of the twins." Said Ayad. Camila gasped.

"Who's the other twin?" She asked. Jasmine looked at her.

"Once, in the middle of the night, we got attacked by two men. They ran away with the baby-the other twin. We caught them and told them to return the baby or we would call the police-we would call the police either way anyways. They said ..." Jasmine stopped speaking. Ayad carried on.

"They said they would take us to court, saying we were abusing and mistreating the baby. That we were abusing it.

"When they took us to court, they didn't exactly believe the men, but they didn't believe us either. The men got imprisoned-they still are, but they said it was dangerous for us to take care of the baby. They had no proof that we were harmful parents. But then I guess the world isn't always fair."

"They were even gonna take Camila." Said Aziz.

"I remember that."

"Yes," said Jasmine.

"But we didn't let them. We didn't have any choice about the other baby though. She's this one." Jasmine pointed at the baby Ayad was holding in the picture

"But... well..." Jasmine was speechless all of a sudden. Something wasn't right. Something bad had happened to that baby, for definite, something that seemed to be still troubling Jasmine. I don't know why, but something told me this was the right time to see the locket.

To explain what *really* happened. I ran upstairs. I heard Camila asking if she should come after me. I got the locket I got the locket out of my cabinet and ran back downstairs. I sat down and opened the locket. It wasn't very clear. I held it up to the light. And there it was. 'My beloved wife, with my sister and her husband and their children: *Aziz, Ali, Sumayyah, Camila, Aleena.*

Aleena. Wasn't that *me*? At the back was the same picture as the one in Ayad's hand.

"My brother gave it to you." Said Jasmine, stunned. "Did you look at it earlier?"

"No, just now," I said.

"Well, I guess that what I was trying to tell you. You've always been a part of us, just far, far away. You're my daughter, and were all happy the way it is now."

I squealed and gave my mum a hug. It happened. I really found my real family. And I was the happiest girl. Everybody gathered round. I was no longer an orphan child. I belonged and was loved.

Now I know who I am.